~~Breaking~~ Making Up

Two original stories in one unique collection
by
Miranda Lee and Susan Napier

Revenge is a powerful emotion—love's
wrongs always beg to be righted. But
vengeance has its price, as each character in
this exciting collection of two brand-new
romances soon discovers!

Be enticed and involved by dangerous
desires, share the passion of bittersweet
seductions, as two irresistible men from
Down Under—one an Australian, the other
a New Zealander—find the time has come to
settle old scores. Will these gorgeous guys
win the women they've always wanted?

Turn the pages and find out!

MIRANDA LEE is Australian, living near Sydney. Born and raised in the bush, she was boarding-school educated and briefly pursued a classical music career before moving to Sydney and embracing the world of computers. Happily married, with three daughters, she began writing when family commitments kept her at home. She likes to create stories that are believable, modern, fast paced and sexy. Her interests include reading meaty sagas, doing word puzzles, gambling and going to the movies.

SUSAN NAPIER was born on Saint Valentine's Day, so it's not surprising she developed a never-ending love of romance. She started her writing career as a journalist in Auckland, New Zealand, trying her hand at romance fiction only after she married her handsome boss! Numerous books later she still lives with her most enduring hero, two future heroes—her sons!—two cats and a computer. When she's not writing, she likes to read and cook, often simultaneously!

MIRANDA LEE
SUSAN NAPIER

Br~~eaking~~ Making Up

Harlequin Books

TORONTO • NEW YORK • LONDON
AMSTERDAM • PARIS • SYDNEY • HAMBURG
STOCKHOLM • ATHENS • TOKYO • MILAN
MADRID • WARSAW • BUDAPEST • AUCKLAND

ISBN 0-373-11907-0

BREAKING/MAKING UP

First North American Publication 1997.

BREAKING/MAKING UP © Harlequin Books S.A. 1997.
SOMETHING BORROWED © 1992 by Miranda Lee.
VENDETTA © 1995 by Susan Napier.

Printed in U.S.A.

CONTENTS

MIRANDA LEE

Something Borrowed

CHAPTER ONE

'JAMES hasn't seen your dress, has he?' Kate asked, glancing at the magnificent satin and lace bridal gown hanging on the wardrobe door. 'You know that's considered unlucky.'

Ashleigh put down her mascara and smiled at her chief bridesmaid in the dressing-table mirror. 'No, Miss Tradition. He hasn't. Not that it would worry me if he had,' she added with a light laugh. 'You know I don't believe in superstitions. *Or* fate. *Or* luck. People make their own luck in life.'

Kate rolled her eyes. 'You've become annoyingly pragmatic over the years, do you know that? Where's your sense of romance gone?'

It was killed, came the unwanted and bitter thought. A lifetime ago...

Ashleigh felt a deep tremor of old pain, but hid it well, keeping her mascara wand steady with an iron will as she went on with her make-up.

'Just look at you,' Kate accused. 'It's your wedding-day and you're not even nervous. If I were the bride my hand would be shaking like a leaf.'

'What is there to be nervous about? Everything is going to go off like clockwork. You know how organised James's mother is.'

'I wasn't talking about the wedding. Or the reception. I was talking about afterwards... You know...'

'For heaven's sake, Kate,' Ashleigh said quite sharply. 'It's not as though I'm some trembling young virgin. I'm almost thirty years old, and a qualified doctor to boot. My wedding-night is not looming as some terrifying ordeal.'

Oh, really? an insidious voice whispered at the back of her mind.

Ashleigh stiffened before making a conscious effort to relax, letting out a ragged sigh. 'I'm sorry,' she apologised. 'I shouldn't have snapped at you like that.'

'You *are* nervous,' her friend decided smugly. 'And you know what? I think it's sweet. James is a real nice man. Much nicer than...' Kate bit her bottom lip and darted Ashleigh a stricken look. 'Oh, I...I'm sorry. I didn't mean...I...'

'It's all right,' Ashleigh soothed. 'I won't collapse in a screaming heap if you mention his name.'

'Do you...ever think of him?' Kate asked, eyes glittering with curiosity.

Too damned often, came the immediate and possibly crushing thought.

But Ashleigh gathered herself quickly, refusing to allow Jake—even in memory form—to mar her wedding-day.

'Jake's as good as dead as far as I'm concerned,' she stated quite firmly. 'As far as *everyone* in Glenbrook is concerned. Even his mother doesn't speak of him any more.'

'What about James?' the other girl asked. 'I mean...he and Jake are twins. Doesn't he ever talk about his brother?'

'Never.'

Kate frowned. 'I wonder what Jake would think of his quieter half marrying his old girlfriend. Does he know, do you think? They say some twins, especially identical ones, have a sort of telepathy between them.'

Ashleigh's fine grey eyes did their best to stay calm as she turned to face her old school-friend. 'Jake and James never did. As far as Jake knowing...' She gave a seemingly offhand shrug. 'He might. His mother insisted on sending him a wedding invitation. God knows why, since she doesn't even know where he's living now. She posted it to his old solicitor in Thailand, who once promised to pass on any mail. Naturally, she didn't receive a reply.'

Ashleigh sucked in a deep breath, then let it out slowly, hoping to ease the constriction in her chest. 'Jake wouldn't give a damn about my marrying James, anyway,' she finished. 'Now...perhaps we'd better get on with my hair. Time's getting away.'

Kate remained blessedly silent while she brushed then wound Ashleigh's shoulder-length blonde hair into the style they'd both decided on the previous day. Even though Ashleigh appeared to be watching her hairdresser friend's efficient fingers, her mind was elsewhere, remembering things she shouldn't be remembering on the day she was marrying James.

Jake...holding her close, kissing her.

Jake...undressing her slowly.

Jake...his magnificent male body in superb control as he took her with him to a physical ecstasy, the like of which she doubted she would ever experience again.

A shiver reverberated through her.

'You're not cold, are you?' Kate asked, frowning.

Ashleigh tried to smile. 'No... Someone must have walked over my grave.'

Her friend laughed. 'I thought you didn't believe in stuff like that. You know what, Ashleigh? I think you're a big fibber. I think you believe in fate and superstitions and all those old wives' tales as much as the next person. And I'll prove it to you before this day is out. But, for now, sit perfectly still while I get these pins safely in. I don't want to spear you in the ear.'

Ashleigh was only too happy to sit still, her whole insides in knots as a ghastly suspicion began to take hold. Was she marrying James simply because of his physical likeness to Jake? Could she be indulging some secret hope that, when James took her to bed tonight, her body would automatically respond the same way it had to his brother?

She hadn't thought so when she'd accepted James's proposal. Ashleigh believed she was marrying him because he was the only man she'd met in years who seemed genuinely to love her, whom *she* liked enough to marry, and who wanted what she was suddenly wanting so very badly: a family of her own. Sex had not seemed such an important issue.

Now...with her wedding-night at hand...it had suddenly become one.

Perhaps she should have let James make love to her the night he'd asked her to marry him. At least then she would have known the truth. Looking back to that occasion, she had undoubtedly been stirred by his unexpectedly fierce kisses. Why, then, had she pulled back and asked him to wait? Why? What had she been afraid of? As she'd said to Kate...she was hardly a trembling virgin.

Ashleigh mentally shook her head, swiftly dismissing the possibility that her body—or her subconscious—*might* find one brother interchangeable with the other. She had *never* confused James with Jake in the past. Others had, but never herself. The two were totally different in her eyes, regardless of their identical features.

They'd been in the same class at school since kindergarten, she and Jake and James, though the boys were almost a year older than her. The three had been great mates always, spending all their spare time together. It

wasn't till the end of primary school that their relationship
had undergone a drastic change. The three of them had
seemed to shoot up overnight, Jake and James into lithe,
handsome lads, and Ashleigh into a lovely young woman
with a figure the envy of every girl in Glenbrook.

By the time they had finished their first year in high
school the more extroverted, aggressive Jake had staked
a decidedly sexual though still relatively innocent claim
on Ashleigh. She'd become his 'steady', and from then
on James had taken a back seat in her life, even though
she had always been subtly aware that he was equally
attracted to her, and would have dearly liked to be in his
brother's shoes.

But she'd had eyes only for Jake.

How they had lasted till their graduation from high
school before consummating their relationship was a minor miracle. Oh, they'd argued about 'going all the way'
often enough, with Jake sometimes becoming furious with
her adamant refusal to let him. But she had seen the way
other teenage boys talked about girls who gave sex freely,
and had always been determined not to give in till Jake
had proved he wanted her for herself, not her nubile
young body.

Ashleigh almost smiled as she remembered the first
time Jake had made real love to her, the day after her
eighteenth birthday, two weeks after they'd graduated.
What an anticlimax their first effort had been. Jake had
been furious with himself, knowing he'd been too eager,
too anxious.

'Too damned arrogant and ignorant,' were *his* words.

Jake had gone out then and there and bought a very
modern and very progressive love-making manual, then
quickly became the most breathtakingly skilful lover that
any mortal male could become, mastering superb control

over his own urgent young body, thrilling to the way he'd eventually learnt to give the girl he loved such incredible pleasure.

Or so Ashleigh had romantically imagined at the time. She should have known that it was just Jake being his typical obsessive self. She certainly should have begun to doubt the depth of Jake's love when he announced in the New Year that he was going overseas—*alone*—for a couple of months. She'd stupidly believed his story about his rich Aunt Aggie's giving him the holiday as a reward for his great exam results and insisting he go immediately, saying it would broaden his mind for his future writing career. He'd promised Ashleigh faithfully to be back in time to go to university with her in March.

But by March Jake had been in prison in Bangkok, awaiting trial for drug trafficking and possession, after trying to board a plane home with heroin in his luggage. Though greatly distressed, Ashleigh had flown over to support her boyfriend, certain he was innocent. The penny hadn't dropped till after Jake had been found guilty and given a life sentence. He had looked her straight in the eye from behind those filthy bars and told her quite brutally that *of course* he was guilty. What in hell did she think he'd really come over for?

But it had been his subsequent personal tirade against her that had shattered Ashleigh completely. His cruelly telling her that he had grown out of their puppy love during his weeks abroad; that he found her blind faith during his trial suffocatingly laughable; that she was boring compared to the *real* women he'd enjoyed since leaving home and that he didn't want to see her pathetic face again, let alone receive any more of her drippy, mushy love letters.

Ashleigh had returned home to Australia in a state of deep despair and disillusionment, having had to defer her entry into medical school till the following year due to her emotional state. In truth, she had almost succumbed to a nervous breakdown over Jake. Yet still some mad, futile hope had made her keep on writing to him. Not love letters. Just words of forgiveness and encouragement. Every day she had gone out to the mail box, hoping against hope for a letter back.

It had never come.

In the end, she'd crawled out of her crippling depression and gone on without Jake.

But the scars left behind from her disastrous teenage romance had plagued her personal life, spoiling every relationship she'd tried to have. Always she'd compared the man with Jake. His looks, his personality, his drive, his lovemaking...

They'd all failed to measure up. Which was crazy! For what had Jake done to her? Let her down. Let his family down. Let *everyone* down.

'What made you come home to Glenbrook to practise medicine?' Kate asked all of a sudden, startling Ashleigh from her reverie. 'From what you've told me, you were doing well down in Sydney.'

'Very well,' Ashleigh agreed. 'But the city can be a lonely place, Kate, without your family or someone special to share your life. I remember I spent my twenty-ninth birthday all alone, and suddenly I was homesick. Within a week I was back here in Glenbrook.'

'And in no time you found James. God, life's strange. There you were in Sydney for years, where there must be hordes of handsome, eligible men, and what do you do? Come home and find your future hubby in good old Glenbrook.'

'Yes...' Ashleigh recalled the night she'd answered an emergency call from the Hargraves home where Mr

Hargraves senior had unfortunately suffered a fatal heart attack. It had been James who'd opened the door...

'I suppose there's no hope of you-know-who coming back to town, is there?' Kate probed carefully.

'I wouldn't think so. It's been over three years now.'

Three years since the Thailand government had unexpectedly pardoned a few foreign prisoners during a national celebration—one of them being Jake—and Ashleigh had still foolishly started hoping he'd come home to her.

Well, he had come home all right. For less than a day, apparently, his visit only to ask for money before he went back to the very country that had almost destroyed him! He hadn't come to see her, even though she'd been home at the time.

One would have thought that such callous indifference should have made it much easier for Ashleigh to see other men in a more favourable light. But somehow...it hadn't.

A type of guilt assailed Ashleigh. James deserved better than a bride who spent her wedding-day thinking about another man, especially his own brother.

She gave herself another mental shake. She wouldn't do it any more. Not for a second! And if tonight there were fleeting memories of another time, and another lover, she would steadfastly ignore them.

I will be a good wife, she vowed. The very best. Even if I have to resort to faking things a little...

'Well, what do you think?' Kate asked after one last spurt of hair-spray.

Ashleigh swallowed, then glanced in the mirror at the way her wayward blonde hair was now neatly encased in a sleek French roll. 'That's great,' she praised. 'Oh, you're so clever!'

'*You're* the clever one, Dr O'Neil,' came her friend's laughing reply.

A hurried tap, tap, tap on the bedroom door had both women glancing around. The door opened immediately and Nancy Hargraves, James's mother, hurried into the room.

'Goodness, what are you doing here, Nancy?' Ashleigh exclaimed, getting to her feet. 'Has something gone wrong? Don't tell me it's raining down at the park!'

The actual ceremony was to take place in a picturesque park down by the river, James having vetoed his mother's suggestion they have the wedding at a church neither of them attended. Ashleigh had happily gone along with his idea of a marriage celebrant and an open-air wedding, choosing the local memorial park as a setting. Nancy, though not pleased, had acquiesced, warning them at the time that if it rained it would be their own stupid fault!

'No, no, nothing like that,' she muttered now in an agitated fashion.

Ashleigh was surprised at how upset James's ultra-cool and composed mother seemed to be. Her hands were twisting nervously together and she could hardly look Ashleigh in the face.

'Could I speak privately to Ashleigh for a minute or two?' she asked Kate with a stiff smile.

'Sure. I'll go along and check that the others are nearly ready.' The others being Alison and Suzie, Ashleigh's cousins—the second bridesmaid and flower girl respectively.

'Thank you,' Mrs Hargraves said curtly.

Kate flashed Ashleigh an eyebrow-raised glance before leaving the room, being careful not to catch the voluminous skirt of her burgundy satin bridesmaid's dress as she closed the door behind her.

Ashleigh eyed her future mother-in-law with both curiosity and concern. It wasn't like Nancy to be so flustered. When she'd offered to help with the wedding arrangements Ashleigh had very gratefully accepted, her own mother having died several years before. She imagined not many women could have smoothly put together a full-scale wedding in the eight weeks that had elapsed since the night she'd accepted James's proposal. But Nancy Hargraves had for many years been Glenbrook's top social hostess, and all had been achieved without a ruffle.

Ashleigh got slowly to her feet, taken aback to detect red-rimmed eyes behind the woman's glasses.

'What's happened?' she said with a lurch in her stomach.

'I...I've heard from Jake,' came the blurted-out admission.

Ashleigh felt the blood drain from her face. She clutched her dressing-gown around her chest and sank slowly down on to the stool again. It was several seconds before she looked up and spoke. 'I presume he rang,' she said in a hard, tight voice. 'There's no mail on a Saturday.'

The other woman shook her head. 'He sent me a letter through a courier service. It arrived a short while ago.'

'What...what did he say?' she asked thickly.

'Apparently the wedding invitation only just reached him,' Nancy said with the brusqueness of emotional distress. 'He...he sends his apologies that he can't attend. He...he also sent this and specifically asked me to give it back to you today *before* the wedding.'

Ashleigh stared at the silver locket and chain dangling from the woman's shaking fingers. Her own hand trembled as she reached out to take it, a vivid memory flashing into her mind.

'What's this?' Jake had asked when she'd held the heart-shaped locket out between the bars of his cell the night before the verdict had come down.

Her smile had been pathetically thin. 'My heart,' she'd said. 'Keep it with you while you're in here. You can give it back to me when you get out, when you come to claim the real thing.'

'I could be here for years, Leigh,' had come his rough warning. Jake always called her Leigh, never Ashleigh.

'I'll wait...I'll wait for you forever.'

'Forever is a long time,' he'd bitten out in reply. But he'd taken her offering and shoved it in the breast pocket of the shabby shirt he'd been wearing.

Now she stared down at the heart-shaped locket for a long, long moment, then crushed it in her hand, her eyes closing against the threatened rush of tears.

'I'm sorry to have upset you, Ashleigh,' Nancy said in a strained voice. 'I know what Jake once meant to you. But believe me when I say I wanted nothing more than to see you and James happily married today. I did not want to come here with this. But I had to do what my son asked. I just *had* to. I...'

She broke off, and Ashleigh's wet lashes fluttered open to see a Nancy Hargraves she'd never encountered before. The woman looked grey, and ill.

Anger against Jake flooded through her, washing the pain from her heart, leaving a bitter hardness instead. How dared he do this, *today*, of all days? How *dared* he?

Ashleigh pulled herself together and stood up, the locket tightly clasped within her right hand. 'It's all right, Nancy,' she stated firmly. '*I'm* all right. I have no intention of letting Jake spoil my wedding-day. Or my marriage. You haven't told James about the letter, have you?'

Nancy's blue eyes widened, perhaps at the steel in Ashleigh's voice. 'N...no...'

'Then everything's all right, isn't it? I certainly won't be mentioning it. By tonight, James and I will be driving off on our honeymoon and he'll be none the wiser.'

She was shocked when her future mother-in-law uttered a choked sob and fled from the room.

CHAPTER TWO

ASHLEIGH stood there for a few moments in stunned silence, her thoughts in disarray. But she soon gathered her wits, renewing her resolve not to let Jake spoil her marriage to James. No doubt Nancy would soon collect herself as well and present a composed face at the ceremony in little over half an hour's time.

'Mrs Hargraves gone, I see?' Kate said as she breezed back into Ashleigh's bedroom. 'What on earth did she want? She looked rather uptight.'

'Yes, she did, didn't she?' Ashleigh agreed with a deliberately carefree air. Kate was a dear friend but an inveterate gossip, the very last person one would tell about the correspondence from Jake. Everyone in Glenbrook would know about it within a week, with suitable embellishments. It had been Kate who had furnished Ashleigh with the news of Jake's fleeting visit over three years before, the information gleaned from Nancy Hargraves's cook, a talkative lady who had her hair done at Kate's salon every week.

Ashleigh smiled disarmingly at her friend. 'It proves that even someone like James's mother can be nervous with the right occasion. I thought something must have gone wrong there for a moment. But she just called in to give me this to wear today.' And she held up the locket and chain. 'Must be one of your mob, Kate. An upholder of old traditions. This is to be my *something borrowed.*'

The irony of her excuse struck Ashleigh immediately, but she bravely ignored the contraction in her chest. She'd lent Jake her heart, and now he'd given it back to her.

Good, she decided staunchly. I'll entrust it to James. He'll take much better care of it, I'm sure.

With a surge of something like defiance, she slipped the chain around her neck. 'Do this up for me, will you?' she asked her chief bridesmaid.

'Will do. But what are you going to do for the something old, something new and something blue?'

'No trouble,' Ashleigh tossed off. 'My pearl earrings are old, my dress is new, and my bra has a blue bow on it.'

'Spoil-sport,' Kate complained. 'I had a blue garter all lined up for you.'

'OK. I'll wear that too. Now help me climb into this monstrosity of a dress, will you? The photographer's due here in ten minutes.'

'You're suitably late now, Miss O'Neil, ' the chauffeur of the hire-car informed. 'Shall I head for the park?'

'God, yes,' her father grumbled from his seat beside her. 'If we go round this damned block one more time I'll be in danger of being car-sick for the first time in my life!'

'Kate insisted I be at least ten minutes late,' Ashleigh defended, feeling more than a little churned up in the stomach herself. But it wasn't car-sickness. Much as she had maintained a cool exterior since the perturbing encounter with Nancy, inside she was a mess. And it was all Jake's fault. The whole catastrophe of her personal life so far had been Jake's fault!

But no longer, she decided ruefully. She was going to marry James and be happy if it killed her!

She slanted her father a sideways glance, thinking wryly that he was far from comfortable in his role as father of the bride. He was a good doctor, but an antisocial man, whose bedside manner left a lot to be desired.

Ashleigh believed she'd contributed a lot to his practice since joining it, always being willing to lend a sympathetic ear, especially to women patients. They certainly asked for her first. She planned to continue working, at least part-time, even if she did get pregnant straight away, which was her and James's hope.

Thinking about having a baby, however, brought her mind back to the intimate side of marriage, and the night ahead of her. Another attack of nerves besieged her stomach. Dear heaven, she groaned silently. She hadn't realised that going to bed with James would loom as such an ordeal.

Her hand fluttered up unconsciously to touch the locket lying in the deep valley between her breasts.

Any worry over her wedding-night was distracted, however, when the park came into view. Oh, my God, she thought as her eyes ran over what Nancy had arranged for her favourite son's wedding.

A rueful smile crossed Ashleigh's lips. James's vetoing a church service clearly hadn't stopped his mother's resolve to have a traditional and very public ceremony. Right in the middle of the park under an attractive clump of trees sat a flower-garlanded dais, with an enormous strip of red carpet leading up to it, on either side of which were rows and rows of seats, all full of guests. But the *pièce de résistance* was the electric organ beside the dais, which seemed to have a hundred extension leads running from it away to a van on which two loud speakers were placed.

Ashleigh shook her head in drily amused resignation.

Serve herself right for giving James's mother *carte blanche* with the arrangements.

'Trust Nancy Hargraves to turn this wedding into a social circus,' her father muttered crossly as the white Fairlane pulled up next to the stone archway that marked the entrance to the park. A fair crowd of onlookers were waiting there for the bride's arrival, not to mention several photographers and a video cameraman. 'Thank God I've only got one daughter. I wouldn't want to go through all this again.'

Ashleigh felt a surge of irritation towards her father. Why did he always have to make her feel that her being female was a bother to him?

If only Mum were still alive, she thought with a pang of sadness. She would have so loved today. Not for the first time Ashleigh wondered how such a soft, sentimental woman had married a man like her father.

People always claimed she took after her mother. She certainly hoped so.

'I've been thinking,' Edgar O'Neil went on curtly while they sat there waiting for the chauffeur to make his way round to Ashleigh's door. 'It's as well Stuart will be joining the practice next year. You're going to be too busy having babies and dinner parties to be bothered with doctoring. And rightly so. A woman's place is in the home.'

Ashleigh was too flabbergasted to say a word. She had always known that her father was one of the old brigade at heart. Also that her younger brother would be joining the practice after he finished his residency. But her father spoke as if her services would be summarily dispensed with!

As for her giving dinner parties...Nancy Hargraves and her late husband might have been the hub of Glenbrook's social life, the Hargraves family owning the logging company and timber mill which were the economic mainstays of the town. But James was not a social animal in the least, and Ashleigh didn't anticipate their married life would contain too much entertaining.

She had planned to go on working, babies or not. Or at least she *had*…till her father had dropped his bombshell just now. Her heart turned over with a mixture of disappointment and dismay, though quickly replaced by a prickly resolve. She would just have to start up a practice of her own, then, wouldn't she?

Alighting from the car, Ashleigh had to make a conscious effort to put a relaxed, smiling face on for the photographers and all the people avidly watching her every move. Heavens, but it looked as if the whole town had turned out to see their only lady doctor getting married.

Or was there a measure of black curiosity, came the insidious thought, over her marrying the wrong brother?

Stop it! she breathed to herself fiercely. Now just you stop it!

'Doesn't she look beautiful?' someone whispered as she made her way carefully up the stone steps and through the archway, her skirt hitched up slightly so she didn't trip.

'Like a fairy princess,' was another comment.

Ashleigh felt warmed by their compliments, though she knew any woman would look good in what she was wearing. The dress and veil combined had cost a fortune, Nancy having insisted she have the very best. Personally she had thought the *Gone With The Wind* style gown, with its heavy beading, low-cut neck, flounced sleeves and huge layered skirt, far too elaborate for her own simpler tastes. But Nancy had been insistent.

'It's expected of my daughter-in-law to wear something extra-special,' she had said in that haughty manner which could have been aggravating if one let it. But Ashleigh accepted the woman for what she was. A harmless snob. James had a bit of it in him too, but less offensively so.

Jake had been just the opposite, refusing to conform to his mother's rather stiff social conventions, always going his own way. Not for him a short back and sides haircut. Or suits. Or liking classical music. Jake had been all long, wavy hair, way-out clothes and hard-rock bands. Only in his grades had he lived up to his parental expectations, being top of the school.

Irritation at how her mind kept drifting to Jake sent a scowl to her face.

'Smile, Doc,' the photographer from the local paper urged. 'You're going to be married, not massacred.'

Ashleigh stopped to throw a beaming smile the photographer's way. 'This better?'

'Much!'

'Come, Ashleigh,' her father insisted, taking her elbow and shepherding her across the small expanse of lawn to where the imitation aisle of red carpet started and her attendants were waiting. 'We're late enough as it is.'

Her chief bridesmaid thought so too, it appeared. 'Now that's taking tradition a bit too far for my liking,' Kate grumbled. 'I was beginning to think you'd got cold feet and done a flit.'

'Never,' Ashleigh laughed.

'Well, stranger things have happened. But all's well that ends well. I'll just give the nod for the music to start and the men to get ready. I think they're all hiding behind the dais. Still nervous?' she whispered while she straightened her friend's veil.

'Terrified,' Ashleigh said truthfully, a lump gathering in her throat as all the guests stood up, blocking out any view of the three men walking round to stand at the base of the dais steps.

'Good. Nothing like a nervous bride. Nerves make them look even more beautiful, though God knows I don't know how anyone could look any more beautiful than you do today, dear friend. James is going to melt when he sees you.'

'Will you two females stop gasbagging?' the father of the bride interrupted peevishly.

'Keep your shirt on, Dr O'Neil,' Kate returned, not one to ever be hassled by a man, even a respected physician of fifty-five. Which could explain why, at thirty, she'd never been a bride herself. 'We'll be ready when we're ready and not a moment before. Your father's a right pain in the neck, do you know that, Ashleigh?'

'Yes,' came the sighing reply.

The organ started up.

Kate grinned. 'Knock 'em dead, love.'

'You make this sound like the opening night of a show,' Ashleigh returned in an exasperated voice.

Kate lifted expressive eyebrows, then laughed softly. 'Well, it is, in a way, isn't it?'

Heat zoomed into Ashleigh's cheeks.

'Aah,' the other girl smiled. 'That's what I wanted to see. The bridal blush. She's ready now, Dr O'Neil.'

As ready as I'll ever be, Ashleigh thought with a nervous swallow.

The long walk up the red carpet on her father's arm was a blur. The music played. Countless faces smiled at her. It felt almost as if she were in a dream. She was walking on clouds and everything seemed fuzzy around the edges of her field of vision.

Only one face stood out at her. Nancy's, still looking

a little tense, and oddly watchful, as though expecting Ashleigh to turn tail and run at any moment.

And then the men came into view…

First came James, looking tall and darkly handsome in a black tuxedo, his thick, wavy hair slicked back neatly from his well-shaped head. And next to him was…

Ashleigh faltered for a moment.

For the best man *wasn't* Peter Reynolds, the new accountant at Hargraves Pty Ltd and James's friend since college, but a perfect stranger!

Her father must have noticed at the same time. 'Who the hell's that standing next to James?' he muttered under his breath to her.

'I have no idea…' The man was about thirty with rather messy blond hair, an interesting face and intelligent dark eyes. After a long second look Ashleigh knew she'd never seen him before in her life.

Her eyes skated down to the other groomsman. Stuart, her brother. He smiled back reassuringly, after which she swung her gaze back to James. Their eyes locked and for one crashing second Ashleigh literally did go weak at the knees. For James was looking at her as if she were a vision, an apparition that he could scarcely believe was real, as if he couldn't tear his eyes away from her.

All thought of mysterious best men fled, her breath catching at the undeniable love and passion encompassed within James's intense stare. He'd never looked at her like that before, even when he'd said she was the only woman he'd ever loved, the only woman he could bear marrying. His stunningly smouldering gaze touched her heart, moved her soul. *And* her body.

Ashleigh was startled to find that suddenly the night ahead did not present itself as such an ordeal after all. Her eyes moved slowly over her husband-to-be and her heart began to race, her stomach tightening, a flood of sensual heat sweeping all over her skin.

The raw sexuality of her response shocked her. She hadn't felt such arousal since…since…

Quite involuntarily one trembling hand left her bouquet to once again touch the locket.

James's deeply set blue eyes zeroed in on the movement—and the locket—and her hand retreated with guilty speed. Surely he didn't know anything about the locket, did he? Surely Nancy hadn't told him about it, and the letter from Jake?

James was frowning now, all desire gone from his gaze.

'Keep moving, Ashleigh,' her father ordered in an impatient whisper.

Haltingly she took the remaining few steps that drew her level with the still frowning James. For a second she didn't know what to do, where to look, but as she gazed up into James's face she was distracted from her emotional confusion by the dark circles under his eyes. She peered at him intently through her veil, and saw how tired and strained he looked, as though he hadn't had much sleep the night before.

A possible solution to the mystery of the missing best man catapulted into her mind. Peter had taken James out on a stag night last night, *against* everyone's advice. Maybe they'd really tied one on and something had happened to Peter in the process. A severe hangover, perhaps?

James reached out his left hand towards Ashleigh. Still rattled, she almost took it without first handing her bouquet over to Kate. Turning to do so, she caught a glimpse of Kate and the others, staring and frowning, first at the strange best man, then at her. Ashleigh shrugged, handed the bouquet to Kate then turned back to place her hand in James's. When his right hand moved to cover it she looked down and almost died, her mouth falling open as she stared down at the bruised knuckles, the badly grazed skin.

Her eyes flew to his. 'James,' she husked. 'What happened to your hand? What—?'

'Ssssh,' he hushed. 'Afterwards... The celebrant's ready to start.' And he urged her up on to the wide step, where they would be in full view of the guests.

'We are gathered here today to celebrate the marriage of...'

Ashleigh found it hard to concentrate on the ceremony, her head whirling with questions. The image of James in a physical fight was so out of character that she couldn't even think of what possible reason there could be for it. And whom had he been fighting with, anyway? Surely not Peter?

Peter was even less physically inclined than James, being older and much slighter in build, as well as a connoisseur of the finer things in life. Art...the theatre...fine wines... Ashleigh often wondered what he was doing in a small timber town like Glenbrook. He didn't appear to like the place any more than he liked *her*.

Not that he ever said as much openly. But she had seen the coldness in his eyes when he looked her way, and he rarely let an opportunity go by to slip in a mildly sarcastic comment about women in general, even though Ashleigh knew they were really directed at one woman in particular. Namely herself.

In fact, Peter Reynolds was the one dark cloud on the horizon of her future with James, one made all the darker because she hadn't been quite able to pin down the reason for his antagonism towards her. Usually she got on well with men on a social level. Better than with women, who seemed threatened by her being a doctor.

Except for Kate, of course, Ashleigh thought warmly. Kate was never threatened by anything.

'Till death us do part.'

'A tight squeeze on her fingers snapped Ashleigh back to the present.

'I...I do,' she said shakily, and flashed James an equally shaky smile.

He didn't smile back.

Ashleigh stared. At his grim mouth; his hooded eyes; his clenched jaw.

It was at that moment she realised something was dreadfully wrong. James had not been involved in some silly male spat with Peter after drinking too much. It was something much more serious than that. Not only serious. But somehow dangerous.

To her...

CHAPTER THREE

PANIC clutched at Ashleigh's insides, making her heart-rate triple and her thoughts whirl.

But not for long. Ashleigh was a logical thinker and she quickly calmed down, accepting that she was being ridiculous and fanciful. The events of the day so far had clearly unnerved her.

James would *never* do anything to hurt her, or cause her to be in any danger. She was mad to even think so. He was too kind, too caring, too gentle. As for his having been in a physical brawl with Peter... The very idea was ludicrous! There had to be some other reason for his damaged hand. Certainly something *had* happened to Peter, but probably no more than the hangover she'd first envisaged. Meanwhile she refused to let her imagination run away with her.

Lifting her chin slightly, she turned her eyes to the front. But, despite all her inner lectures, an uneasy churning remained in her stomach.

A long shuddering breath of self-exasperation trickled from her lungs, which brought a sharp glance from the groom, *and* the celebrant, who was about to start James's vow.

She let her eyes drop away from both of them, staring uncomfortably at the floor while the celebrant's deep male voice rolled on.

'Do you, John James Hargraves, take...?'

Ashleigh's eyes jerked up, her lips parting in protest. For John James was what *Jake* had been christened, the exact reverse of James's names.

But as the celebrant continued, loud and clear, she reconciled herself to the mistake and shut her mouth again. Why make a fuss? These things happened all the time at weddings. Nevertheless, she hoped James didn't mind the mix-up.

Apparently not, for his 'I do' at the end was strong, even if there was a decided raspiness in his voice.

The doctor in Ashleigh automatically diagnosed that he was getting a cold—the result, no doubt, of a heavy night out and whatever else James had been up to last night. *Truly*, she thought somewhat irritably, never being at her sympathetic best when it came to male drinking bouts, let alone indulging in one the night before getting married.

Ashleigh was mulling over this uncharacteristic lack of consideration in her husband-to-be when James reached out and abruptly took her left hand, almost crushing her fingers within his as he drew it across her towards him. Her eyes flew up in startled alarm, meeting his steely blue gaze with a definite contraction in her chest.

This was a side of James she had certainly never seen before—a tougher, harder, much more macho side. It came to her astonished self that perhaps he was more like Jake than she'd realised.

And why wouldn't he be? inserted the voice of ruthless reason. They were identical twins, weren't they? They had probably started out with identical natures, till the stronger of the two personalities stamped his presence more loudly, forcing the other to adopt a more passive, compromising role. Maybe, once Jake had gone from the Hargraveses' household, James had been able to crawl out from under the shell his brother's dominance had forced around him, even though the gentle, less assertive manner he'd adopted over the years had by then become a habit.

Today, however, the pressure of the wedding and the mishap over Peter was probably bringing his basic male aggression to the fore.

To be frank, Ashleigh wasn't sure if she liked this more masterful James or not. Perhaps she didn't want to be faced with the prospect of his becoming more and more like Jake. Perhaps she was more comfortable with their remaining totally different.

'The ring?' the celebrant asked of the best man.

The stranger with the fair hair and dark eyes extracted the ring from his pocket and handed it over. Only the one ring. James had resisted Ashleigh's attempts to make him wear one, saying he didn't like to wear jewellery of any kind. Which was quite true.

Lifting her hand, he began sliding the wide gold band on to her ring finger, saying the traditional words as he did so. 'With my body I thee worship...'

Ashleigh's heart caught at the fierce emotion James was putting into his vow. Unless, of course, it was the oncoming cold bringing that huskily thickened quality to his voice.

Her eyes lifted to his and she knew instantly that that was not so. The earlier steel had melted to a swirling blue sea of desire, drawing her gaze into its eddying depths, seducing her with the silent promise of a passion she had never dreamt James capable of. But it was there in the eyes holding hers, in the hand wrapped securely around her fingers, in the chemical electricity which was surging from his hand to hers.

'And with all my worldly goods I thee endow,' he concluded, his eyes dropping to caress first her softly parted lips, and then her lush cleavage.

Ashleigh was shocked, a shaming heat stealing into her cheeks. Surely this was not the right moment for open seduction?

Flustered, she yanked her hand away from James's disturbing touch, not daring to look at him in the process. Instead, she concentrated her regard on the celebrant, who cleared his throat and announced pompously, 'I pronounce that they be Man and Wife together.' Beaming widely at them both, he added, 'And now, Mr Hargraves, you may kiss your lovely bride.'

Oh, God, Ashleigh thought with a flip-over of both her stomach and heart. Instant nerves had her holding her breath as James turned her to face him before slowly lifting the thin layer of netting back over her head. Quite deliberately she didn't look up into his eyes, focusing her attention on his chin. But slowly and inexorably her eyes were drawn upwards till they were right on his mouth. She watched, heart pounding, as those well-shaped lips opened slightly.

And then he was bending his head.

Ashleigh froze till contact was made, suppressing a gasp of dismay to find that his lips were oddly cold and lifeless on hers. Somehow, after his smouldering scrutiny, she'd been expecting—no, *hoping*—for more. A possessive, hungry kiss. An explosion of passion. A sample of what was to come.

But when James's mouth lifted from hers she was left feeling desolate, a jagged sigh of disappointment wafting from her lungs.

The sigh brought another incisive glance from her brand-new husband. This time Ashleigh wasn't quick enough to avoid returning his look.

There was no longer any promise of seduction in his silent stare, only an unreadable implacability that sent a deep shiver reverberating through her. For, though the expression in his eyes seemed impassive on the surface, there was a razor's edge lurking within those cool blue depths. One got the impression of suppressed violence, of wild forces, barely tamed behind a civilised façade.

Ashleigh had a vivid mental picture of James tonight, ripping her clothes from her then taking her with a savagery bordering on rape. She sucked in a startled breath, her glossed lips gasping apart, her breasts rising and falling in a bemused agitation, caused as much by her own reaction to such a vision as the vision itself.

Was she appalled, or aroused?

If the latter, how could that be? She had never been a woman to indulge in rape fantasies. She had consistently shrunk from sexually aggressive men over the years. They reminded her too forcibly of Jake, who, though never violent, had exploited her own sexual vulnerability towards him with a frightening ruthlessness.

Would James turn out to be of the same ilk?

Her agitation was just about to rocket into fully fledged panic when the dangerous light disappeared from his gaze and he was turning away from her to accept his best man's congratulations, leaving Ashleigh wondering if she was imagining things again.

Of course you are, her high degree of common sense argued, seemingly for the umpteenth time that day. James is a gentleman. A *gentle* man. Now you stop this nonsense this very second!

But it still crossed Ashleigh's mind as the celebrant led the wedding party up on to the dais for the signing of the marriage certificate that not once, so far this afternoon, had James smiled at her.

Now that wasn't like him at all!

While the adolescent James had been a shy, sensitive

lad who didn't make friends all that easily, especially with girls, maturity had developed in him a more relaxed, easy-going personality which was quietly successful with women. In fact, there wasn't an attractive girl in Glenbrook who hadn't at some stage been dated by the very eligible and handsome James Hargraves.

He had, however, gained a reputation for being a bit fickle, never staying with one girl for too long. It had also been rumoured that he had a mistress stashed away some-where, accounting for his many weekends spent away from the town, probably in Brisbane or the Gold Coast. Though Glenbrook was in New South Wales, it wasn't far across the Queensland border, and only a couple of hours' drive to that state's capital and the nearby tourist Mecca of Surfer's Paradise.

But the weekends away had lessened with the added responsibility that fell on James's shoulders after his father's death, and Ashleigh hadn't given James's supposed mistress—or his sex-life—a single worrying thought.

Till now...

Could he still be seeing this woman occasionally? Was that why he had almost meekly accepted her wish not to make love before their marriage?

Unsettling doubts besieged her, but she quickly brushed them aside. Any reason James had for seeing another woman would no longer be valid after tonight. She would make sure of that! Meanwhile, she *did* need to have ex-plained some of the things that had bothered her this af-ternoon. Peter's absence and James's hand, as well as his swinging moods.

'James,' she whispered as they sat down side by side at the special signing table. 'You must tell me what's going on.'

'Regarding what?' he said slowly, turning an annoyingly bland face her way.

'What happened to Peter, for one thing?' she went on agitatedly.

Now James smiled, a sardonic grimace that did nothing to ease Ashleigh's peace of mind. 'You might say Mr Reynolds and I didn't see eye to eye on a particular subject,' he muttered.

'You mean me, don't you?'

He nodded. 'I found it necessary to impress on him quite forcibly that it would be in his best interests to leave Glenbrook forthwith.'

Ashleigh's mouth fell open. 'Then you did...hit him?'

James's smile showed great satisfaction. 'Several times.'

'Oh, my goodness... Oh, James...I'm so sorry.'

'Don't be. I enjoyed it.'

'You...*enjoyed* it?'

James must have seen her shock, for his hand moved swiftly to cover hers, his eyes holding hers with the first real warmth and affection he'd bestowed on her since she'd arrived today. 'Forget Peter. He's not worth thinking about.'

She jumped when Kate touched her on the shoulder. 'You're supposed to be signing,' her friend said with a teasing laugh, 'not having an intimate little tête-à-tête. Keep that for later.'

James flashed Kate a smile that was more like his usual self, and Ashleigh let out a long-held breath.

'Whatever you say, Kate,' James agreed. 'Has Rhys explained about Peter's sudden attack of appendicitis?'

Ashleigh only just managed to stifle her astonished gasp at this cool delivery of the obviously prearranged excuse. Goodness, but James was constantly surprising her today.

Who would have thought so many faces were hiding behind his usually bland faade?

'Yes. It was a real shame, wasn't it?' Kate returned with blithe indifference. Peter Reynolds was not one of her favourite people, either. 'You were lucky to have someone else to step in at the last minute who could fit into Peter's clothes.'

'You're so right. Well, let's get on with this.' And, picking up the pen, he started to sign.

Ashleigh stared down over his shoulder with a peculiar feeling of tension invading her chest. When she saw the words 'James John Hargraves' form in James's usual conservative hand an unmistakable wave of relief flowed through her, bringing a measure of exasperation. For heaven's sakes! What had she been expecting?

'Smile, Mrs Hargraves,' Nancy's hired photographer said, crouching down in front of the desk and snapping away. 'Now one while you're signing...'

Finally she was finished, and settled back in her chair to watch both Kate and this Rhys person sign, happy for her heartbeat to get back to normal.

It was impossible to mind Peter's not being one of their witnesses, as she was only then realising how much she'd despised the man. Still, she couldn't imagine what he'd said or done to turn James against him so vehemently. They'd been such close friends for so long. But, whatever it was, she sure as heck hoped James had smacked him one right on his supercilious moosh.

Yes, now that she'd had time to mull it over, she wasn't at all upset by this turn of events.

The substitute witness finished signing, startling her with a surprisingly warm smile as he turned to step away from the desk. She got the oddest feeling he knew a darned sight more about her than she did about him. When the celebrant also stepped up to put his name to the official documentation of her marriage Ashleigh glanced down at the best man's signature. Rhys Stevenson…

A jab of recognition tickled her brain. The name was familiar. But why? She glanced over her shoulder to where he was standing, talking very amiably to Kate. No, she didn't recognise him at all, yet the name still rang a vague bell.

'I'm sorry I have to dash away,' the celebrant was saying, a widely apologetic smile on his face. 'But I have another engagement this evening and you were—er—a little late getting here. My hearty congratulations, and I hope everything turns out very well. Might I say you both did splendidly? No one would have guessed that—'

'All finished here?' Rhys interrupted, leaving Ashleigh wondering what it was no one would have guessed. 'You have to go now, don't you, Mr Johnson?' he directed at the celebrant. 'You did a great job. A really great job.' He pumped the man's hand then pressed an envelope into it, which no doubt contained the prearranged fee. A big one, judging by Mr Johnson's huge grin as he departed.

A triumphant wedding march suddenly burst forth from the nearby speakers.

'Shall we go, darling?' James said, getting to his feet. Smiling, he picked her bouquet up from where it was lying on the table and handed it towards her.

Ashleigh took it with a trembling hand, his calling her darling leaving her unexpectedly breathless. It was not an endearment James had ever used with her before, but, goodness, the word had sent a ripple of sexual response quivering down her spine.

And what's wrong with that? came the voice of logic. He's your husband now. And, after tonight, your lover…

With a little shiver she hooked her arm through his

offered elbow and allowed herself to be propelled down the dais steps and along the red strip of carpet to the clapping and congratulations of the guests.

Ashleigh would have liked to dive straight into the waiting Fairlane, but she was obliged to go through the motions of posing for photographs in various locations around the park, all the while hotly aware of her new husband beside her, of his hand taking her hand, of his arms encircling her waist, his eyes on hers every now and then.

Yet every time she felt her pulse-rate leap it was accompanied by the most peculiar stab of dismay. For with this new and unexpected desire for James she was irrevocably and finally abandoning what she'd once felt for Jake. For how could she pretend to herself that she still treasured her teenage love while she yearned for his brother's body?

She couldn't, she finally accepted. This would be the end of Jake. The real end. Once she physically surrendered herself to James, there would be no going back, even in her mind.

The thought depressed, then confused her. But then...a lot of things had confused her today. Maybe that was the prerogative of nervous brides.

But she gave voice to one of her minor confusions as soon as they were semi-alone in the back of the hire-car and on the way to James's house for the reception. 'Who is this man Rhys Stevenson? I have the strangest feeling I should know him.'

'He's an up-and-coming Australian film director. You've probably seen his name on the screen, or on television, and absorbed it subconsciously.'

'But how did you meet him and what was he doing at our wedding?' she persisted, not entirely satisfied. 'Don't tell me he was invited, because I saw the list of guests and he wasn't on it.'

'I asked him personally, only a couple of days ago. Lucky I did, as it turned out,' he finished drily.

'Well, yes, but—'

'Are you going to talk about Rhys all the way to the house?' James interrupted, startling her by disposing of her bouquet on to the floor then sliding an arm around her waist and pulling her close. 'I'd much rather tell you that you're the most stunningly beautiful woman God ever put breath into,' he rasped, 'and then do this.'

There was nothing cold and lifeless about his kiss this time. Far from it...

Ashleigh found it difficult, however, to forget the chauffeur behind the wheel, who was possibly watching then in the rear-view mirror. She squirmed under the hot possession of her husband's mouth and hands, an embarrassed heat flushing her cheeks.

Squirming, however, was not the best activity for a woman in the close embrace of a man she'd been becoming more sexually aware of all day. Her chest rubbed against his dinner-suit jacket, a button scraping harshly over one already hardening nipple.

Her lips fell open in a silent gasp, and immediately James's probing tongue found its mark, filling her mouth with a hungry thrust that sent the blood whirling in her head. Dazed, she clung to the lapels of his dinner-jacket, and all thoughts of chauffeurs vanished. There was only that ravenous mouth crushed to hers, and its insatiable tongue, feeding on the sweetness it found behind her own panting lips.

When James finally abandoned her mouth it was to kiss her neck, to mutter unintelligible words against her flushing skin. Ashleigh's head tipped back in a raw response, her whole body drowning in a flood of warmth and heat. The drum-beat of desire began pounding in her heart, and her head, making her oblivious to her surroundings, making her a willing victim to her husband's passion. Already James's mouth was back on hers, taking her down deeper and deeper into maelstrom of need and yearning.

'Damn it,' he rasped when the car turned the corner that led up the hill to his home. 'We won't be staying at this reception late,' he growled. 'I've already waited too long for this night. Far too long.'

Ashleigh shivered at the darkly intense resolve in James's voice and face. But it was a shiver of excitement, not fear. She wanted him as much as, if not more than, she'd ever wanted Jake. Such a realisation ripped through all her preconceived ideas on what she felt for the two brothers. Before it had been love and desire for one. Liking and respect for the other. Now Ashleigh was forced to accept this wasn't so any longer. She had *never* felt this kind of desire before without love. That was why no man had ever reached her since Jake, simply because she'd never loved any of them.

She lifted a trembling hand to James's face and held it there, tears swimming in her eyes. 'I love you, James,' she whispered. 'I really, really love you.'

His head jerked back and he stared at her. For a second Ashleigh was taken aback, unsure if the frozen mask on his face meant he was appalled, or merely deeply sceptical. With a sigh of understanding she realised it had to be the latter.

'I know I said I didn't love you when I agreed to marry you,' she rushed on in a low whisper as the car pulled into the long driveway that led up to the Hargraveses' house. 'To be brutally honest, I thought that, underneath, I was still in love with Jake.'

She felt the muscles in his jaw flinch, though his eyes didn't waver.

'There's been no one else, you see, and I always believed...' Her hand trembled against his skin. 'But, when you kissed me just now and I responded the way I did, I knew it had to be true love.'

There was no doubting the relief that zoomed into those blue eyes, or the emotion behind the husky, 'I knew it. I *knew* it!'

And he kissed her again, deeply and hungrily.

He only released her when the car pulled up at the house. 'Just as well,' she murmured with an embarrassed laugh. 'If we keep this up I'll get your cold.'

'My...cold?' His puzzlement was only momentary. 'Oh, you mean my raspy voice. Don't concern yourself, my darling. It's not a cold. Let's say I—er—did a fair bit of shouting last night and it affected my vocal chords. Now, take that frown off your lovely face and don't let that bastard Reynolds spoil things for us.'

Ashleigh blinked her amazement. That bastard Reynolds? Astonishing. Only last week James had been telling her what a wonderful friend Peter had always been and how grateful he had been for his help with the financial side of the company since his father's death.

She might have liked to take the discussion further— such as exactly what Peter had said to cause the blow-up between them—but the chauffeur's opening the back door for her to get out put paid to that. Putting her hand in the chauffeur's, and a blush of lingering embarrassment on her face, she alighted at the base of the wide steps, glancing up at the house where she would have to live for a while till she and James found something suitable around Glenbrook in which to set up their own home. Perhaps something with enough room for her to have a small attached practice, she thought, since Nancy would hardly let her turn any of the Hargraveses' home into a surgery.

Two-storeyed and in a Cape Cod design, the house had a setting suited to the family's status in Glenbrook, grandly overlooking the town from the crest of a hill. Tall English trees stood in elegant clumps of shade over the surrounding lawns, upon which a large marquee had been erected for the reception.

The guests had not yet arrived, but soon the nearby area would be full of parked cars. Even the photographer hadn't made it yet, having stayed behind to snap some more pictures of the bridesmaids and guests.

All of a sudden Ashleigh recalled what James had said to her in the car, about how they would leave the reception early. She turned to watch him stride around the white Fairlane to join her, a splendid male figure in his tuxedo, his well-tailored clothes highlighting his wide-shouldered, lean-hipped frame.

He caught her staring at him, and an amazingly confident smile caressed his mouth. It jolted her. For there had only ever been one male who'd been so sexually sure of himself with her. Only one...

'Jake,' she whispered on a breathless note, and her fingers fluttered up to the locket.

But the man beside her wasn't Jake. It was his brother, his brother who had finally taken Jake's place in every possible way...

James had stiffened at her uttering his brother's name. He stared down at her, then at the locket, the muscles twitching in his strong jaw. Ashleigh stopped breathing, certain now that he suspected the locket had something to do with Jake. Which was why he had stared at it earlier on.

She opened her mouth to try to explain why she'd chosen to wear the thing today, but he cut her off.

'Do not speak that name again,' he rasped, 'or I won't be responsible for what happens.'

He drew in then expelled a ragged breath.

'Now,' he went on sternly, 'go inside and replace your lipstick. The others will be here soon and it wouldn't do for everyone to think I'd been ravaging you already. My mother, particularly, might find that thought…unnerving. She isn't quite herself today, as I'm sure you've already realised.'

It was at that precise moment that Ashleigh realised James knew not only about the locket, but Jake's letter as well.

CHAPTER FOUR

'You know, don't you?' Ashleigh confronted James. 'About Jake's writing to your mother, about his sending me back this locket?'

James's blue eyes grew watchful beneath a dark frown. 'I am acquainted with my mother's visit to you before the wedding,' he admitted slowly.

'Good God!' Ashleigh gasped. 'Why did she have to tell you? What point was there?' She shook her head in agitation. 'I suppose you think I wore this damned thing because I was still pining for Jake. I wasn't. I wore it in defiance of his rotten arrogance and lack of tact in wanting me to have it on the very day I was marrying his brother!'

'I see,' James said somewhat drily. 'To be honest, I would not have thought of that reason.'

'It's the truth.'

'I don't doubt you.'

'You did believe me when I said I loved you, didn't you, James?'

There was no mistaking the flash of painful irony in his eyes. 'I think you might be a touch confused, my dear, in these unusual circumstances. But I'm a patient man. I know I can win your love, even if it takes me the rest of my life.'

Ashleigh was distressed at the bleak intensity behind his words.

'Leave me now, Ashleigh,' he went on brusquely.

'There are cars coming up the hill. I'll stay out here and greet the guests and organise things for the photographs while you fix your face. Someone will be up shortly to collect you.'

Ashleigh didn't want to leave him. She wanted to go on explaining, reassuring. Oh, how she'd hated seeing the hurt in his face, hated feeling the withdrawal in his manner towards her. But she could hardly stand there arguing with him in front of other people, especially with smudged make-up. Reluctantly she turned and made her way up the front steps and in through the open double doors, holding her skirt up as she made her way slowly up to the bedrooms Nancy had set aside for her as a changing-room.

The door was already open and Ashleigh walked in, her mind still on James and the unhappy thought that he didn't believe she really loved him. But she did. She was sure of it! How could she convince him?

Tonight, she decided breathlessly. Tonight she would leave him in no doubt that she both loved and wanted him as she had wanted no other man, not even Jake.

Damn Jake, she thought angrily. Damn him to hell!

With an abrupt movement her hand swept up under her veil and behind her neck, where she fumbled to unclasp the now hated locket. It stubbornly refused to yield, and in the end she reefed it from her neck with a savage yank, the locket spilling on to the parquet floor and sliding under the double bed.

And that was where she left it, tossing the silver chain on to a chest of drawers.

'Something borrowed,' she scorned out loud. 'Something *buried* would be more like it!'

Ashleigh counted to ten till her breathing was back to normal, then quite deliberately turned her back on the chain and gazed with satisfaction at her going-away outfit, all laid out ready for her on the double bed, complete with shoes and handbag.

It was an elegantly simple suit in emerald-green silk, which hugged her tall, shapely figure and proclaimed to the world that she was all woman. James would like it, she was sure. And in the packed suitcase of clothes already in the boot of James's Jaguar, awaiting their honeymoon, was an ivory satin négligé set that would make any man sit up and take notice, let alone the man who already loved her.

Picking up the black leather handbag, she carried it over to the corner dressing-table, where she opened it and drew out the make-up she'd put in there. First she touched up her foundation, then replenished her blusher and lipstick. She was just applying some perfume when Kate knocked on the open door and breezed in.

'There you are, Ashleigh. James sent me to get you. Hmmm, perhaps I could do with some more lipstick too. May I?'

'Be my guest.'

'The photographer wants to take a few shots in the garden,' Kate explained as she applied the deep pink shade to her wide mouth. 'He spied that clump of rhododendrons and thinks they'll make a splendid backdrop. There...all done...' She looked at herself critically in the mirror, then shrugged. 'Oh, well, we can't all be gorgeous. Come, oh, beautiful bride,' she said, and linked arms with her friend's. 'Your panting groom awaits!'

Laughing, the two friends made their way down the sweeping staircase and out into the mild autumn air, Ashleigh immediately expressing her gratitude that all the guests seemed to have disappeared into the marquee, and weren't waiting to besiege her on the front lawn.

'You have James to thank for that,' Kate informed her.

'I also heard him sneakily instructing the drink waiters to ply everyone with as much liquor as they could handle to keep them out of our way while the official photographs were being finished. By the time we make our grand entrance they'll be high as kites on sherry and a quite lethal fruit punch. I know: I sampled it.'

'I could do with a shot of something lethal myself,' Ashleigh said drily. Kate's ebullience hadn't totally distracted her from how she had left James a little earlier. Neither could she forget that in a couple of hours she would be driving off on her honeymoon with a husband who didn't really believe his bride loved him.

'I could do with sitting down as well,' she continued with a sigh. 'I didn't exactly have a chance to break in these shoes before today, and they're killing me.'

'Ditto repeato,' Kate groaned expressively.

Both girls looked at each other and laughed again.

'Just as well we didn't decide to become models, eh, Kate?'

Kate made a face. 'Well, I didn't have much option on that count, being five feet two and having a face that *didn't* launch a thousand ships.'

'You have a *great* face,' Ashleigh insisted, stopping to look at her friend. And she did, all her big, bold features combining well to present an arresting, vivacious image.

Kate beamed with pleasure at the compliment. 'You are so good for my self-esteem, do you know that?'

'Will you two giggling Gerties mind shaking a leg?' James called over from where the rest of the bridal group were waiting impatiently beside the pink rhododendrons. 'We're all dying of dehydration and hunger here.'

Ashleigh was astonished and relieved to see that James was actually smiling at her. Gone was his earlier scowl, his look of pained anguish. He was a totally different man, confident and positive in his manner. She heaved a happy sigh. Everything was going to be all right after all.

Walking quickly over, she slipped a loving arm through his, smiling up into his face. Clearly her gesture startled him, for he stared back down at her for a second before expelling an exasperated though good-natured sigh.

'Right,' the photographer announced. 'Everyone facing front and smiling.'

'Wait!' Kate shouted, making everyone jump. She rushed over and started straightening Ashleigh's veil where it had caught slightly on some beading on her shoulder. Suddenly she stopped and frowned down at Ashleigh's bare neckline. 'What happened to the locket?' she asked.

Ashleigh groaned silently. Trust Kate to notice and comment. She opened her mouth to voice an excuse, but nothing came to mind, and she was left looking like a flapping flounder.

'It broke,' James said coolly from beside her. 'In the car.'

'Oh, what a pity!'

'Not to worry, Kate,' Ashleigh inserted swiftly, having regathered her wits. 'I still have your garter, which was borrowed as well as blue.'

'A garter?' The new best man perked up. 'How quaint. Can I see it?'

'Certainly not while it's on,' James intervened firmly.

Rhys laughed. 'How possessive you are! But rightly so. Your bride is as lovely as you described to me. I fully understand you now, dear friend. Some things are worth any sacrifice.'

Flattered and flustered, Ashleigh lifted startled eyes to her husband, catching the end of a harsh glare thrown his best man's way.

'Do you think we could get on with this, folks?' the photographer sighed.

The session seemed interminable, as was having to keep on smiling. By the time it drew to an end Ashleigh's mouth was aching. She was also harbouring the beginnings of a headache.

'Something wrong, darling?' James murmured from her side when she put a hand to her temple.

'Only a very small headache,' she smiled softly, thinking that she did so like his calling her that.

'I'll get you something for it. Kate! Take Ashleigh over to that garden seat there while I rustle up some aspirin. Or do you need something stronger?' he directed back at his bride.

'Well...panadol is kinder to the stomach.'

His mouth curved into a wry smile. 'Of course. Doctor knows best.'

She flinched, knowing how men didn't like to be corrected, or told things by a woman. She could never tell her father or brother anything—even about medicine—without earning a reproachful glare or a sarcastic remark. 'Sorry,' she murmured.

'Don't be. I'm proud of your being a doctor. Kate? The seat, please. Be back shortly.' And, flashing them a parting smile, he strode off.

'I didn't realise James could be so masterful,' Kate remarked as she led Ashleigh in the direction of the shaded seat. 'It's very attractive on him, isn't it? I mean, being nice is all very well, but a man shouldn't be too, *too* nice. If he is people walk all over him, including his wife, and then he might lose her respect, don't you agree?'

Ashleigh did.

'Rhys is a very interesting man too,' Kate raved on. 'I

could talk to him all day. The places he's been and the people he's met! Fantastic!'

'Don't tell me you've finally met a man you didn't want to put solidly in his place,' Ashleigh said, amazement in her voice.

'I can't imagine anyone putting Rhys Stevenson in his place.'

'Kate! I do believe you're smitten.'

'Not at all. Just jealous.'

'Of what?'

'Of his lifestyle.'

'Well, we can't all be movie directors!'

'Why not, if that's what we'd like to be?' she said quite aggressively.

Ashleigh stopped and stared at her friend.

'Now don't go giving me one of those looks of yours,' Kate huffed.

'What looks?'

'Oh, your "one must keep one's feet firmly on the ground" looks. Life is meant to be lived, Ashleigh. And I'm not so sure I want to live the rest of mine in good old Glenbrook! Oh, forget it,' she grumbled. 'You wouldn't understand. Not only do you have a rewarding career, but you've just married a great bloke whom it's quite clear you're mad about—and who's mad about you—so what would you know about frustration?'

Suddenly she smiled, a sort of brave, sad smile that caught at Ashleigh's heart. She hadn't realised her dear friend was so unhappy. One would never have guessed. She so wished there was something she could do.

'Just listen to me,' Kate laughed, but it had a brittle edge to it. 'As if this is the right moment to be pouring out all my worries and woes. Now come along and sit down before I get into trouble for not doing as his lord and master commanded. Heavens, if I didn't know different I might have thought it was Jake telling me what to do. Remember how he used to boss us around at school?'

'Yes, Kate,' Ashleigh said stiffly. 'I haven't forgotten. But I'm *trying* to.'

'Oh…oh, sorry, love. God, me and my big mouth. Is your headache very bad? I guess I haven't made it any better by my whingeing then bringing up ancient history. Truly, Ashleigh, I'm a real clot. Forgive me?'

Ashleigh patted her friend's hand. 'Of course, but I would rather you not talk about Jake, especially in front of James. It's rather a sore point between us, I'm afraid.'

'I won't, believe me. The James I'm seeing today might just bite my head off. Aah…here he is now…'

'Nurse Hargraves to the rescue,' he said mockingly, and pressed the glass of iced water he was carrying into her free hand. 'Now…give me that infernal bouquet and hold out your other hand,' he commanded.

She did, and he dropped two white tablets into her palm.

'Swallow them up straight away. I know you medical people. Great at dosing others but rotten at taking things yourself. Gone? Good. Look, I'm sorry, but we'll have to make an appearance in the marquee. Mother is making unhappy noises.'

Ashleigh was surprised to find she quite enjoyed the feeling of being cosseted, not having had that experience since her mother died. Leaving the empty glass behind on the garden seat, she allowed James to walk herself and Kate over to the marquee, a lovely, warm sensation spreading in the pit of her stomach at having his solicitous arm around her waist.

If this was what being married to James was going to be like then she was all for it. Being married to *her* seemed to be good for him too. As Kate had rightly observed, James wasn't usually so quick to take control of situations, to taking the role of leader. Yes, he certainly was coming out from under the shadow of his brother and being his own man. And suddenly Ashleigh no longer minded.

'Oh-oh,' James whispered in her ear. 'Brace yourself. Here come the aunts and uncles and various assorted cousins to tell you how beautiful you are and how lucky I am. You'll have to kiss the men too. Convention, you know. And we must uphold all the social conventions,' he added quite testily. 'Mother would have a seizure if we didn't!'

It wasn't till they'd finally taken their adjoining seats at the main bridal table under the huge tent that a puzzling thought struck Ashleigh. James never called his mother 'Mother'. He always called her Nancy. Neither was he in the habit of using that caustic, almost cutting tone when speaking about her foibles.

A deep frown settled on to her high, wide forehead as she tried to fathom out why she was so bothered by that, since the reason for it was clear enough. Mother and son had clearly had an argument that morning about Jake's letter—hence Nancy's agitation and tears—and James was taking his anger out on her by being disdainful and aloof.

Yet it *did* bother her. Quite considerably. Perhaps because she wanted her wedding-day to be a really happy occasion.

'James,' she whispered, and he leant her way, pressing his whole side against hers.

A shivery charge zoomed through her body. 'Please don't be cross with your mother,' she said thickly.

The muscles along his arm stiffened. 'What makes you think I'm cross with her?'

'You don't usually call her "Mother" like that, for one thing. And you were...well, you were sarcastic when talking about her. That's not like you.'

'I see,' he murmured thoughtfully. 'And what would you like me to do about it?'

'Go and talk to her and make up. She looks so unhappy.' Which the woman did, not a smile having passing Nancy's thinnish lips all day.

'Mmmm...well, we can't have that, can we?' he muttered in a voice that didn't sound as conciliatory as Ashleigh might have hoped.

He got to his feet and strode off in the direction of his mother, leaving Ashleigh feeling oddly perturbed.

'God, it *is* good to be sitting down,' Kate pronounced from her right-hand side. 'Where's James off to?'

'Has to see his mother about something,' came her suitably vague answer.

'I have to give Mrs Hargraves credit where credit it due,' Kate said. 'This is all top-drawer stuff. Genuine lace tablecloths, real silver cutlery, candelabras, the finest crystal glasses. We might be out under a circus tent—if you can recognise canvas through the decorations—but it could well be a king's banquet table, judging by the accoutrements.'

Ashleigh agreed that Nancy had pulled out all stops in making sure that her son's wedding had no equal in the history of Glenbrook. Right at this moment two hundred happy, suitably intoxicated guests were busy finding their silver-embossed place-names at one of the twenty lace-covered tables, while a small orchestra played subtle wedding music and silver, white and burgundy streamers and balloons fluttered over their heads. A four-tier wedding cake stood proudly on its own table to one side, patiently awaiting its part in the celebration that was about to start.

The caterers were hovering, clearly wanting to serve the first course of the meal.

Ashleigh was still glancing around when her eyes landed on James talking to his mother in a far corner. They were too far away for her to see the expressions in their eyes, but their body language reeked of a barely controlled anger, Nancy making sharp movements with her head and hands while she spoke. James's fists were balled at his side, his broad shoulders held stiffly while he stood silently and listened. Suddenly James launched into speech, and Nancy's head rocked back, as though his words were like a physical blow. She stared back at him while he raved on, her face frozen.

At last he finished speaking and they simply stood there, eyeing each other, both still obviously livid, each one seemingly waiting for the other to break first.

It wasn't James.

Quite abruptly Nancy leant forward and kissed her son on the cheek, after which she plastered a smile on her face and went about her hostess duties with the sort of serenely smiling look on her face one might have expected from Nancy, but which had been absent all afternoon.

The whole incident rattled Ashleigh, especially with James making his way swiftly across the room towards her with a black look still on his face. What on earth was going on with those two? She could understand that initially James wasn't pleased with his mother's having taken a returned gift from his brother to his bride on her wedding-day, especially when that same bride had once been besotted with that brother.

But surely, with her having discarded the locket, James could see that Jake was not going to be a threat to their relationship? Why couldn't he forgive and forget? But no, she thought irritably, he was a typical male, whose anger was not allowed to be so quickly discarded.

Ashleigh was initially astonished when, just as suddenly as his mother, James appeared to pull himself together and adopt a more pleasant expression. Yet as he drew closer there was no mistaking the hard glint remaining in his eyes, or the tension in his stiffly held arms and shoulders. Though, once he became aware of Ashleigh's reproachful eyes upon him, he shrugged and smiled.

'I'm afraid she's still not pleased with me,' he confessed on sitting down beside her, 'but she's agreed to play her part a bit more convincingly.'

'Play her part?' Ashleigh repeated, frowning. 'Isn't that an odd way of putting it? Your mother *loves* you, James. She wouldn't want there to be bad feeling between you. She—'

'For God's sake, don't start worrying about *her*,' he suddenly snapped. 'She'll survive.'

Ashleigh fell silent, truly shocked by his manner.

'Hell,' he muttered. 'This is even harder than I thought it'd be.'

Ashleigh stared at him. 'What...what do you mean?' she asked, totally perplexed.

He turned to lock eyes with her, his gaze penetrating and deep. 'Do you trust me, Ashleigh?' he rasped, his voice low and husky.

A dark, quivery sensation fluttered in her stomach.

'Of...of course...'

'Then don't give my mother's attitude a second thought. Take no notice of anything she says or does. Believe me when I say she isn't concerned for *your* happiness. *Or* mine. That's all you have to remember.'

'But...but...that doesn't make any sense.' Which it

didn't. Nancy *adored* James. He'd always been the apple of her eye.

'I know. That's why I asked for your trust. Do I have it?' he demanded to know.

'I...'

'Do I have it?' he repeated in an urgent tone.

Ashleigh's heart started to pound and she knew that, with her answer, her fate would be sealed, irrevocably. Her mind flew to what she'd told Kate earlier that day, about not believing in destiny or one's fate being outside a person's own control. She still believed that. Her husband, in asking her for blind trust, was really testing her love for him, as well as her faith in the person he was.

There was really only one answer she could give.

'Yes,' she said firmly.

'Then just do as I ask,' came James's harsh answer.

Ashleigh was to remember later that night that she had deliberately chosen to place her future in this man's hands. So she had nobody else to blame but herself.

CHAPTER FIVE

'FANCY Kate catching my bouquet,' Ashleigh laughed as James drove down the hill away from the Hargraves home. 'You know what else? I think she and your friend, Rhys, really hit it off. They were chatting away together all evening.'

'I wouldn't be getting my hopes up about Kate and Rhys if I were you,' James returned drily. 'He's an incorrigible chatter-upper of women.'

'Oh?' Ashleigh frowned, a tinge of worry in her voice.

'And I wouldn't worry about your Kate either. If ever there was a female who can take care of herself it's that one!'

'I suppose so...'

'You don't sound convinced.'

'Kate's rather vulnerable at the moment.'

'Aren't we all?' he muttered. 'Aren't we all?'

A strained silence fell between them at this darkly cryptic remark, with James putting his foot down more solidly. The powerful car hurtled into the night, eating up the miles between Glenbrook and their destination.

Ashleigh found herself with time to ponder the not so subtle difference in James today. He was far moodier than his usual easygoing self, far more uptight. Originally she'd put it down to wedding-day jitters, plus irritation at Jake's last-minute correspondence, not to mention his doubts over his bride's really loving him or not.

But now that the reception was over and they were off on their honeymoon Ashleigh began to wonder if there was a far more basic reason. Perhaps he was worried about tonight, about how sex between them would turn out. Was he concerned, perhaps, that she would compare his lovemaking with Jake's? And, more to the point...would *she*?

She honestly didn't know. All day her sexual response to James had surprised and pleased her. But it was one thing to feel a few heart flutters, quite another to experience the sort of abandon during total intimacy that she had experienced with Jake.

Not that it would overly concern *her* if they didn't achieve sexual perfection straight away. Ashleigh was a realist. She knew these things could take time. They had, even with Jake! But she had the awful feeling James would be cut to the quick if he didn't satisfy her tonight, if he thought for a moment he had failed her in bed.

Thinking about his possible disappointment and unhappiness began twisting her insides into knots. Before she could stop it a quavering sigh escaped her lips.

Hard blue eyes snapped her way. 'What's that sigh supposed to mean?' he asked in a definitely suspicious tone.

'Nothing. I...' Suddenly she sat up straight and blinked rapidly. 'James! What...what are you doing?' she gasped.

What he was doing was obvious! He was turning into a motel, a rather cheap-looking highway motel into which they were definitely *not* booked. They were supposed to be on their way to a five-star luxury hotel on the Gold Coast.

'I'm afraid this won't wait, Ashleigh,' he ground out.

Ashleigh turned to stare with wide eyes at the man sitting beside her. How determined he sounded. How...*forceful*.

She swallowed, her mind filling with all those moments today when she'd glimpsed a James she had never seen before, a James simmering with unleashed passion. Clearly he couldn't bear to wait any longer to make love to her. She found his impatience to have her in his arms both flattering and arousing, her pulse-rate accelerating into overdrive, an excited heat flushing her cheeks.

'This isn't like you, James,' she laughed softly as he braked to an abrupt halt in front of the motel office.

His sidewards glance was sardonic. 'I realise that, believe me. Wait here,' he ordered brusquely, and climbed out from behind the wheel. 'I won't be long.'

She watched James stride purposefully into the office to book in, thinking to herself that he had a very attractive walk. Funny, she had never thought that about James before. But as he came back through the door, key in hand, her eyes were drawn to his very male and undeniably impressive body, lingering on the breadth of his shoulders before slowly working her way downwards. She didn't have to wonder what he would look like naked. Mother nature had assured that, as an identical twin, he would have the same well-shaped, muscular, virile body as Jake.

A quivering started deep in her stomach and she knew beyond a doubt that nothing was going to go wrong between them. It was going to be right. *Very* right. *Exquisitely* right. Suddenly she was as anxious as he was to be in bed together, to have the right to touch his hard naked flesh at will, to lie back and accept his body into hers as many times as it would take to assuage her rapidly soaring desire.

She smiled at him when he climbed in behind the wheel, her smile the smile of a siren. It stopped him in his tracks, his eyes glittering blue pools as they locked with hers. 'You shouldn't look at me like that,' he rasped.

'Why not?' she said thickly. 'You're my husband, aren't you? I love you and want you. I'm not ashamed of that.'

His groan startled her, as did his hands, reaching out to pull her towards him, his mouth covering hers with a raw moan of passion. His kiss only lasted a few seconds, but those few seconds burnt an indelible fact in Ashleigh's brain.

This was the man she loved and wanted. Not Jake. James.

They were both gasping when he tore his mouth away, both astonished at what had transpired between them. But somehow James did not seem as happy about it as Ashleigh was. Why that was so she couldn't work out.

He muttered something unintelligible, then whirled away to restart the engine and drive the car round to the motel units behind the main building, parking in front of door number eight. Getting out straight away, he walked briskly around to open the passenger door and help her out.

Ashleigh was slightly disconcerted when his eyes refused to meet hers, also at the way he once again turned away from her quite sharply to insert the key in the door. Pushing it open, he waved her inside.

'But what about our luggage?' she asked, staying where she was.

He went to say something, but just then another car made its way around the back. Shrugging, he went over, opened the boot and brought the two suitcases inside, Ashleigh trailing behind with a frown on her face but a defiant resolve in her heart. As keen as she was for James to make love to her, she was not about to abandon her whole dream of a truly romantic wedding-night.

'I won't be a moment,' she said, snatching up her suitcase and disappearing into the adjoining bathroom. As she closed the door she had a fleeing glimpse of James, standing open-mouthed and exasperated beside the bed.

She was more than a moment. She was a good fifteen minutes, having a shower, powdering and perfuming her body, taking down and brushing out her shoulder-length blonde waves, then finally slipping on the ivory satin full-length nightie.

'Goodness,' she murmured to herself in the *en suite* bathroom's vanity mirror. It hadn't looked quite *this* sexy in the lingerie shop. But then she hadn't had her hair down that day, and neither had her breasts strained against the moulded bodice with nipples like hard round pebbles jutting suggestively through the satin.

Drawing the matching lace and satin robe up her long arms and over her slender shoulders didn't make the underlying nightwear any less sensuous. If anything, half covering up her full-breasted figure made the revealing garment underneath even more tantalising. She was sure that, when she walked, the overlay would flap teasingly open while the satin nightie underneath would cling to her naked stomach and thighs.

Just thinking about how James would look at her in this rig-out had Ashleigh's heart slamming madly against her ribs. But she *wanted* to send him wild with need and desire, wanted him to think of nothing but fusing his body with hers, of thrusting his hardness deep inside her already moistening flesh, of giving himself up to the pleasure she could give him.

She didn't want him to think of Jake.

He was pacing up and down across the room when she emerged, having removed nothing but his jacket and tie. He ground to a halt at the sound of the door opening, his head snapping round to glare at her. But the second his eyes raked over her provocatively clad figure his expression changed, from a black frustration to a smoulderingly stirring desire.

Hot blue eyes started on her face and hair then travelled slowly downwards, Ashleigh's skin breaking out in goosebumps when she saw his eyes narrow on her already aching breasts.

Quite abruptly his eyes snapped back up, shocking her with the anguish in their depths.

'You don't understand, Ashleigh,' he growled, shaking his head. 'The reason I stopped here... It...'

She began undulating towards him, and any further words died in his throat. As she approached she lifted trembling hands to peel the outer robe back from her swollen breasts, letting it slip off her shoulders and flutter to the floor behind her. She kept moving, breathless but confident in her femininity, knowing that with each sinuous movement of her limbs she was ensnaring him in her web of seduction, inflaming his male need to a level that would brook no more hesitation, only action.

She drew right up to him, her lips softly parted, her head tipping back slightly as she wound her arms up around his neck. 'I don't want any explanations,' she husked, her mouth so close to his that she could feel his breath on her lips. 'I just want *you*. Right here and right now...'

Her fingers splayed up into his thick black hair as she leant into him, her breasts pressing flat against the hard wall of his chest.

Once again James surprised her, standing where he was without attempting to touch her back, frozen within a dangerously explosive tension. She could feel it in the corded muscles straining in his neck, in the way his breathing was silent and still. 'You think you know what you're doing, Ashleigh,' he muttered low in his throat. 'But you don't.'

A dark shudder raced through him. 'Hell...I wish I had the strength to deny myself this. But I haven't. It's asking too damned much!'

And, with that, his arms swept up and around her, imprisoning her against him and bending her spine back till her hair spilt free from her neck and her mouth was an open, gasping cavern. His head bent to cover that cavern with hot, ravenous lips, to fill its dark, moist depths with his tongue, to stunningly imprint upon its owner that her mouth was there primarily for his possession, to be used as he willed, to be taken and abandoned only as he ordained.

Or so it seemed. For when she struggled against such an unexpected and confusing display of male mastery—her arms retreating from his neck to push vainly at the solid wall of his chest, her head trying to twist from side to side—one of his hands slid up into her hair, grasping the back of her head and holding it firmly captive. But soon she herself was caught up in her own pleasure, giving in to his physical domination with a throaty moan of surrender.

She shuddered when he finally left her mouth to trail rapid kisses down her throat, dazedly aware she should be appalled by his semi-violence, but conceding she wasn't at all. Instead she thrilled to the savage mouth that nipped and sucked at her flesh, working its way inexorably towards her breasts and their pointed, expectant peaks.

'James,' she groaned when she felt his hot breath hover over one of her aching nipples.

His head jerked up and she stared at him with glazed eyes. 'What's wrong?' she husked in bewilderment.

She could hardly think, her whole being in a world of

its own, where it was responding instinctively, without thought, without reason.

'Nothing,' he growled.

'Then touch me,' she begged. 'Here...' And she brushed a shaking hand over the throbbing tip.

'Oh, God,' he moaned aloud, and bent his mouth to do her bidding, suckling the tender flesh right through the nightie, drawing the whole aureole into his mouth and rubbing the satin-covered nub over and over with his tongue.

Never had she felt such electric pleasure, such tempestuous excitement. Heat swept through her, making her blood race, her limbs grow heavy with desire. She closed her eyes and let the rapture spread, her lips parting, her arms falling limply to her side.

One of his broad hands had settled in the small of her back, the other on the flat of her stomach, moving in a sensual circular motion as his mouth continued to tantalise first one breast, then the other, both bare now, the nightie having somehow been pushed off her shoulders to crumple at her waist, held up perhaps by the hand caressing her stomach.

Ashleigh became hotly conscious of that hand as it moved lower and lower... Of their own accord her legs shifted slightly apart in silent invitation for a more intimate caress. James obliged, his hand sliding between her legs, forcing the satin inwards with him, rubbing the silken material over her arousal till she moaned in utter abandonment and need.

James moved to assuage that need, peeling the nightie down over her hips to pool at her feet while he sank to his knees in front of her, licking the soft flesh of her inner thighs, gradually easing them wider and wider apart till he could move his mouth with exquisite intimacy over her.

Ashleigh caught her breath, her hands shooting up to close over his shoulders lest she fall. For those knowing lips and tongue seemed to know exactly what to do to send her mad, moving hotly over the core of her need before returning again to her most sensitive spot. When her soft moans turned to whimpering little cries he pulled her down on to the carpet with him, kissing her mouth while he freed his desire with frenzied movements.

For several excruciating seconds his head was lifted to look down at her naked arousal, his eyes glittering with satisfaction as they roved over the stark evidence of her passion. For Ashleigh was wanton in her desire for his possession, her body restless and open for him, her womanhood moist and swollen.

With an almost tortured groan he knelt between her legs, and, scooping up her buttocks, impaled her with a single powerful thrust.

Ashleigh gasped, her back arching up from the floor, her arms reaching out for him to come to her in a lover's embrace. He sank down upon her with a jagged moan, gathering her tight against him.

'Oh, my darling, my only love,' he rasped, then began surging into her with a powerful, passionate rhythm. She gasped at the speed with which she found herself on the brink, then moaned as she tumbled headlong into an ecstatic release, the fierceness of her contractions hurtling James into an equally explosive climax that left him shaking uncontrollably.

Ashleigh clasped his trembling body close to her, totally unmindful of the potent seed he'd just spilt deep inside her. She certainly wasn't thinking of how she'd deliberately chosen to have her wedding-day right at her most fertile time of the month so that she might conceive straight away. All she wanted at that moment was to keep her husband's body fused with hers, to wrap her arms and legs tight around him, to kiss his sweat-covered neck, to tell him how much she loved him.

His shirt had come loose from the waistband of his trousers during their torrid mating, and she slipped her hands up underneath with a contented sigh to rove across bare flesh. But, when her fingers encountered the strangest ridges and dips in the skin on his back, she froze. James did not have scars on *his* back. It was smooth and clear and hairless. At least, it *had* been a week ago when they had gone swimming in the pool at his home.

My God! Exactly what *had* happened last night? Had he been in some sort of accident?

'James,' she whispered, her voice shaking, her whole insides shaking. 'What have you done to your back?'

She felt him stiffen, felt his shuddering sigh.

'Nothing,' he muttered. 'It's the same back I've had for years.'

Slowly he withdrew from her, easing himself back to sit on his heels and adjust his clothes. 'You see, Leigh,' he went on, raking her pale face with bleak blue eyes, 'the fact is...I'm not James.'

CHAPTER SIX

ASHLEIGH came as close to fainting at that moment as she had ever done in her life. All the blood drained from her face and for a few black moments her world tilted on its axis.

But the crisis passed, and when it did her first reaction was a desperate denial.

'Don't be ridiculous! Of course you're James. I mean...what are you trying to say?' she laughed shakily, sitting up and snatching the satin nightie from the carpet near by and somehow dragging it over her nude body. 'That you're *Jake*? If this is your idea of a sick joke, James, then...'

His hands shot out to grab her upper arms, his blue eyes steely as he leant over her. 'I *am* Jake. Look at me, Leigh. Really look at me. You know the difference. You've always known the difference. You didn't today because I was where you and everyone expected *James* to be, dressed in James's clothes, my hair cut exactly like James's, acting like James.'

He made a scoffing sound. 'Well...maybe not acting *entirely* like James. Believe me, Leigh, when I say you wouldn't want me acting like him tonight.'

'Stop calling me that,' she screamed at him. 'Stop saying you're Jake. You're not! You can't be! It's impossible! Besides, I...I *hate* Jake! I...'

Her high-pitched hysterical outburst was terminated

abruptly and effectively by his right hand's covering her mouth and pushing her, none too gently, flat on her back on to the carpet.

'Shut up, for God's sake, or we'll have the motel manager knocking at our door. Look, I'm sorry for how things turned out here tonight. I was going to tell you the truth earlier but, God damn it, Leigh, you've only yourself to blame. You virtually seduced me. *Me...Jake...*not James. For, even if you didn't recognise me on a conscious level, your body did subconsciously. It recognised me and responded to me, right from the first moment it set eyes on me in that park. Tell yourself you hate me all you like, Leigh, but deep down you know you don't!'

Once again her face paled, her eyes widening with horror as the truth refused to be denied.

Jake hadn't sent a letter home... He'd come in person...

It had been Jake looking at her with such inflammatory desire during the ceremony...Jake who'd evoked that mad response when he'd kissed her in the car...Jake who'd just made devastatingly rapturous love to her...

She stared up at him, appalled.

His hand lifted from her mouth and he sat back on his heels. 'I see you've finally accepted the facts.'

Confusion and anguish sent her hand careering across his face, slapping it hard. 'You bastard!' she cried brokenly, and then she slapped him again. 'I thought you were James. I would never have let you touch me if I'd known it was you!' She began hitting out wildly with both hands, across his face, his shoulders, his chest.

He grabbed both her wrists and ground them slowly back down on the carpet above her head, both their chests heaving as he pressed down flat on top of her. 'Is that so?' he bit out, blue eyes flashing with a very male anger.

'Well, you know who I am *now*, don't you? I'm Jake. Not James. Let's see how you respond *this* time, shall we?'

'No, Jake, *don't*,' she choked out. But even as his mouth took possession of hers she was quivering with an instant and breathless excitement.

Afterwards she wept, totally shattered by the moans of ecstasy still echoing in her ears.

'Oh, Leigh, darling, don't cry,' he murmured softly, holding her naked body close to his now equally naked body.

She almost surrendered to this unexpected and disarming tenderness, almost let it wash away the bitter shame she was feeling.

But just in time she recalled what had just happened, how he had ruthlessly exploited his knowledge of her body and its sexual weaknesses, how, when she'd been at her most aroused, he'd coerced from her an erotic intimacy she'd once given freely.

'Let me go, you…you…bastard!'

She reefed out of his arms and, scrambling to her feet, dashed into the bathroom, slamming and locking the door behind her. The sight of her reflection in the vanity mirror almost made her sick. She couldn't help staring at her puffy red lips, at her still hard nipples, at the red marks his possessive hands had made all over her flesh.

Shivers ran up and down her spine as she hugged herself in disbelief. This wasn't happening to her, she thought dazedly. It was a nightmare, and very, very soon she was going to wake up.

'Leigh?' Jake called out through the door. 'Are you all right? Answer me, Leigh!'

Groaning, she dashed into the shower, snapping on the water, unmindful that it was cold to begin with. She washed herself feverishly, trying to get every trace of him from her body. But she couldn't erase the memory of her ultimate surrender to what he wanted. Why, she agonised, had Jake always been able to command such total submission from her? Why?

And what of James? she worried. Where was he? What had Jake done to him last night to force him to let him take his place today?

Thinking about James's predicament had the effect of making Ashleigh pull herself together. For there was more than *her* well-being at stake here. Besides, she couldn't go back in time, couldn't wipe out what Jake had made her do. What she *could* do was find out exactly what had happened where James was concerned, then make decisions from there.

By the time Ashleigh emerged from the bathroom, her nakedness covered by a large towel, she looked fully composed. Her cold gaze swept over Jake where he was sitting quietly on the side of the bed, his trousers and shirt back on, though the shirt buttons were not done up. He looked up at her, a frighteningly hard glint in his eyes.

'Can we talk now?' he asked, getting slowly to his feet. '*Properly*?'

'By all means,' Ashleigh returned frostily. 'I'm more than eager to know how you managed to bring off this despicable charade. Just how many people were in on it, besides your sidekick Mr Stevenson?'

Jake's sigh carried exasperation. 'Look, Leigh, I—'

'Just give me the bare facts, please,' she snapped. 'Nothing else.'

His eyes narrowed. 'Very well. My mother was aware of the situation. As, of course, was James and his best man.'

'*Nancy* knew?' Ashleigh gasped. 'And she...let you get away with it?'

A rather bitter smile creased Jake's mouth. 'Mother was only too glad to go along with my suggestions, once I pointed out the alternative.'

'I can't imagine what you could have said or done to force her to go along with such a preposterous and disgraceful idea!'

Ashleigh swayed on unsteady feet as she recalled Nancy's visit before the wedding ceremony, at how dreadfully upset the poor woman had been. Her heart went out to the lady, to what she'd felt then, to what she must be feeling now. How a son could put his mother through such an ordeal she had no idea.

She took a few ragged steps towards him, her face pained. 'How...how could you do such a thing, Jake?' she rasped. 'To your mother? To me? And *why*? You don't love me. You *never* really loved me!'

And then it came to her. His return had nothing to do with love, but possession. She'd once been his, body and soul, and, while he'd been able to stand her moving on to some unknown man, he hadn't been able to bear her marrying his brother, in James enjoying the fruits—so to speak—of what he had sown.

'Oh, my God,' she groaned. 'What have you done with James? You...you've really hurt him, haven't you?'

Jake's eyes grew scornful at her concern for his brother. 'James is fine. At this very moment he is on his way to Europe in the company of his best man.'

She gaped, totally thrown by why James would meekly go off and let Jake pretend to marry her in his stead. 'But *why* did he let you take his place? *Why*?' she groaned, and shook her head in agitation. 'This is all madness. I...I can't take it in...'

'Peter Reynolds is James's lover,' Jake stated flatly.

Ashleigh froze, her mouth dropping open, her head whirling with what Jake had just said.

'James was marrying you as a cover to ensure his social respectability,' he went on. '*And* to have the child he always wanted.'

Ashleigh staggered over to slump down on the side of the bed. She could not speak. She felt nothing but shock and sheer disbelief.

Jake walked over and sat down beside her, picking up her chilled, lifeless hands, covering and warming them with his own. 'I'm sorry to tell you such upsetting news so bluntly, but is there a nice way for news like that? The only comfort I can give you is that he loves you as much as he is capable of loving a woman. I suppose he thought he would be able to successfully consummate the marriage. He told me he kissed you a couple of times and had been aroused enough by them. To be honest, I don't think James is truly gay. He just met the wrong man at the wrong time in his life.'

Stricken, Ashleigh searched Jake's eyes, hoping to see that he was lying. But she could see he wasn't.

'The invitation to your wedding only reached me three days ago,' he explained. 'I was on a type of holiday in the hills, you see, and the letter went all around the giddy-goat in Thailand before reaching me. I've never been so shocked in all my life. Or more upset. I've sacrificed my love for you twice, Leigh, for what I imagined noble reasons. But I could not stand by and see you marry my brother. Surely you can understand that...?'

Ashleigh blinked. She wasn't understanding very much at the moment. Her mind was back on what Jake had just said.

'What...what do you mean, you sacrificed your love for me...twice...?'

But already a suspicion was forming in her mind that startled and dismayed her.

Those beautiful blue eyes clouded for a moment as though some dark memory had leapt from the past to inflict a special kind of torment.

'I wasn't guilty, Leigh,' he rasped. 'Either of trafficking or possessing drugs. The heroin was included in my luggage by a very clever ruse. I told you I was guilty so you would go away, so you would forget me, so you wouldn't waste your lovely young life pining for a man who was facing life imprisonment in a prison system that knew no such thing as parole or mercy...'

A wave of emotion swelled in Ashleigh's heart as she thought of Jake in that filthy prison, making such a noble, heart-rending sacrifice. 'Oh, Jake,' she cried in genuine pity.

'How was I to know that a twist of fate would eventually set me free?' he went on in a thickened voice. 'Or that when I rushed home, hopeful you might still love me, I would once again be waylaid through treachery?'

'*Treachery*?'

'Yes. My parents'. They didn't believe me when I told them I wasn't guilty, you see. They said I had blackened their name, shamed the family. They said I wasn't wanted around Glenbrook.' His laugh was cynical. 'I rather expected my mother to react that way. She'd always been more concerned over what other people thought and said than what her children felt. But Dad really disappointed me. He didn't want me around either. When I asked about you he told me you were engaged to a medical student and that if I cared about you at all I'd go right away and leave you alone.'

'But...but I *wasn't*!'

'I know that now, Leigh. At the time I was shattered.

And torn. I didn't know what to do. One part of me couldn't believe you had forgotten me. I longed to see you, to take you in my arms, to force you to love me. But common sense and decency demanded that if you were going to marry another man I should stay away. But I needed someone else to look me in the face and tell me you didn't care about me any more, someone I could implicitly trust. I went to Brisbane to speak to James, to the address where I was told he was spending the weekend with a friend. Mr Reynolds, as it turned out. It didn't take me long to see which way the land lay there. Naturally, I was shocked, but I tried to be open-minded about it, for James's sake. When I asked him about you and he confirmed what Dad had told me it never occurred to me he could be lying.'

'But *why* did he lie? It's not as though we were having anything to do with each other back then.'

'He obviously wanted me to leave Glenbrook too, because I knew his secret. He was worried I would stay if I thought there was a chance for me with you.'

'Oh, Jake... Do you realise what I thought when I'd heard you'd come home and hadn't even come to see me? Do you have any idea how I felt?'

He drew her into his arms and held her there, her face pressed against his chest. 'I hope you were devastated,' he groaned. 'I hope you wanted to kill me!'

She wrenched away from him and stood up, grey eyes wide with bewilderment. 'But why would you want that?'

'Because it would mean you still loved me as much as I loved you,' he growled passionately. And, getting to his feet, he tried to embrace her again.

But she resisted, her heart and mind racing with a thousand tumbling, mixed-up thoughts. 'Is that what we felt for each other, Jake? Love?'

Clearly he was startled by her querying their relationship. 'Of course... What else?'

She shook her head in genuine dismay. 'I think there are many names one could call what we felt for each other, what we *still* feel for each other. There's an animal chemistry between us, Jake. It burns whenever we get close enough to each other to touch. But is it love?'

'Of course it is, damn it!'

'Was it love that kept you awake nights in that prison, Jake? Was it love tonight when you saw me in that satin nightie? Was it love that had to prove its power a second time, making me do things I didn't really feel comfortable with after all these years?'

Jake grimaced at the memory. 'I'm not proud of that, Leigh. My only excuse is that I was beyond reason, beyond control. I needed you to show me that nothing had changed between us, to bring to life all the things I dreamed about all these long, lonely years without you.'

Ashleigh sucked in a breath. 'Are you saying, Jake, that there hasn't been any other woman since you got out of prison?'

A slash of guilty red burnt momentarily in his cheeks. 'No, dammit, I'm not saying that,' he ground out. 'Hell, Ashleigh, I thought you were lost to me. I thought... For pity's sake, what do you honestly expect? I'm a normal man. Occasionally I've needed a woman in my bed. But that doesn't mean I loved any of them as I loved you, as I *still* love you. Stop trying to make out our feelings are only sexual, damn you!'

'And damn you too, Jake,' she countered fiercely. 'For thinking this was the way to handle the situation with James, for having the arrogance to take his place without telling me, for making love to me here tonight without revealing your identity first, for playing with my life and my feelings as though you're some sort of god who knows best!

'You *don't* know best,' she raved on, whirling away to pace angrily across the room, her hand clutching the towel so that it wouldn't fall. 'You never did!' She spun round to face him from the safety of distance. 'In the first place, you should never have gone on that rotten holiday without me. Then, after you were imprisoned, you should have given me the right to pine for you if I *chose*, to wait for you if I *chose*. Then, when you were released, you should have come to see me, fiancé or no, and once again given me the right to choose my own fate.

'Damn it, Jake!' she cried in real emotional distress. 'I'm not some mindless puppet. I'm an intelligent woman with, I hope, a certain degree of courage and character. Why couldn't you have treated me like one?'

Jake's teeth clenched hard in his jaw. 'Right. Well, to answer your first accusation, that holiday wasn't my idea. It was my Aunt Aggie's. You know she was my only adult confidante in those days. When I told her I wanted to marry you she thought the same as you—that our relationship was just sex. She made me a bargain. Said if I went away for a little while and still wanted to marry you when I came back she would give us some money to get started, to support us while we went through university. But I was not to tell you that. This was to see how *you* felt too after we'd been separated for a while.'

He lifted his chin with an unrepentant air and walked slowly towards her. 'Well, we've been separated over ten years, Leigh, and it hasn't made a scrap of difference to how I feel about you, or you for me. You love me, woman. Stop denying it.'

He took hold of her shoulders and looked down into her eyes. 'As for the rest of your accusations... The truth is, I took James's place today with the best of intentions, thinking I was saving everyone's feelings, yours included. What do you think would have happened in a small town like this if I'd revealed the truth to you last night and the wedding was called off at the last minute? The speculation and gossip would have been horrendous. This way gives us time to work something out for everyone's benefit. Oh, and, by the way, the wedding wasn't a legal union. The celebrant was an actor Rhys employed for the event.'

Ashleigh was truly taken aback. 'An actor?' she gasped. 'But how...why...I mean...'

'He was an innocent enough accomplice,' Jake explained dismissively. 'Rhys told him you and I had been married secretly just before we found out our family had already planned a grand social occasion, and that we didn't want to disappoint them. He was warned to keep his mouth firmly shut, but the idiot almost let the cat right out of the bag at the signing—remember?—till Rhys stepped in.'

'But...but...the certificate...'

'A cheap photostat copy. I've already torn it up. Believe me, Leigh, when I say I didn't enjoy going through that charade of a marriage. You must know that I would have given my eye-teeth to marry you properly and publicly like that. Pretending to be James at your side was excruciatingly difficult. My only concession to my pride was having the celebrant read out John James instead of James John. Hardly anyone knows John is my real name and I knew they'd all think it was just a silly mistake, if they noticed at all. You were the only possible person who'd catch on, but oddly enough you didn't seem to be listening the first time Johnson said it. You were away in another world. Then the second time...'

'I thought it was just human error,' she finished wearily.

'Look, I know I deceived you, but at least I didn't break any laws.'

Ashleigh stiffened and stepped back from his hold. 'Maybe not in a legal sense, but there are moral laws, surely? Just how long had you intended waiting, Jake, before you told me the truth?'

A slash of guilty red coloured his high cheekbones again.

Understanding shocked her. He'd been going to keep it going as long as he could, at least for the duration of their wedding-night. 'That's what you were arguing with your mother about, wasn't it?' she accused shakily. 'The extent to which you were planning on taking the deception. My God, you don't have a conscience any more, do you?'

'I wish to hell I didn't!' Jake shot back at her. 'God dammit, the only reason I pulled in here was because my stupid conscience got the better of me. I was finally going to tell you the whole horrible truth—even if it meant you'd then hate me—but when you came out of that bathroom, looking so bloody beautiful, I couldn't resist you. Sure, I was a little rough that second time and I'm sorry for that. But I'm not sorry for making love to the woman I love. Not one iota. So shoot me down with words, Leigh. Tell me I'm a savage. A barbarian. Call me any names you like. They'll fit. But while you're calling me names have a look at this and think about who and what turned me into such an animal.'

And, stripping off his shirt, he spun round and showed her what his captors had done to him.

Ashleigh could have cried. She lifted trembling fingers to touch his beautiful skin, criss-crossed with the ugly scars of a savage bamboo flogging. And her heart went out to him. What must he have been through, a young, innocent man, wrongly accused and imprisoned for something he didn't do? How on earth could she stay angry with him, faced with such a heart-rending sight?

Impossible.

Which was exactly what Jake intended, she realised when he swung around and took her in his arms again.

'Leigh, darling,' he urged persuasively, 'come away with me...back to Thailand... I have a house there on one of the beaches... You can practise medicine in the villages near by... They're in desperate need of doctors there... You won't want for anything, I assure you. I've—'

'*No*,' she cried out, appalled at how tempted she was to just fall in with his wishes. '*No!*'

She pushed away from him, clutching the towel defensively in front of her. 'My God, Jake, you ask too much! You've always asked too much. I'm not an infatuated teenager any more, you know. I won't come running when you click your fingers. Besides, even if I did still love you—which I'm not at all sure I do!—I can't just drop everything in my life and go off with you like that. I have responsibilities here in Glenbrook. My family depends on me. I have patients here, friends. My *life* is here. You might be able to bum around on some far away beach in a grass hut for the rest of your life, but that's not how I want to live my life. I...I...'

She broke off, flustered by the slow, ironic smile that was pulling at his lips.

'And what do you think you're smiling at?' she threw at him.

'At my lovely Leigh. So grown up now. So liberated. So wrong...'

'I am *not* wrong!'

'Oh, yes, you are, my darling. About so many things. We belong together. We've always belonged together. Fate has decreed it so.'

'I don't believe in fate!'

'Don't you?' Again he smiled that infuriating smile. 'Well, maybe it takes being released from a hell-hole by some incredible miracle to make one believe in such romantic notions. But I don't mind you not believing in fate. I'm quite prepared to trust to your intelligence. And your love for me. I'm sure you'll finally come to the same conclusion I came to this afternoon, Ashleigh O'Neil.'

'Which is what?' she snapped.

'Which is that you're going to become my real wife in the end, come hell or high water.' His smile suddenly faded, replaced by an expression of thin-lipped determination. 'Now go and get dressed. We're going back to Glenbrook, where you can begin seeing for yourself that you're not wanted and loved and needed there as much as I want and love and need you!'

CHAPTER SEVEN

'So! You decided to bring her back, did you?' was Nancy Hargraves's scowled remark when she opened the front door in her dressing-gown. 'I presume she knows who you really are.' She turned a perceptive eye towards Ashleigh, who tried not to colour guiltily, but failed.

Jake's mother gave her a derisive look. 'Well, nothing's changed where you and Jake are concerned, I see,' she bit out. 'You were always his little puppy-dog, running along behind him, licking at his heels. I suppose you even believe all his protestations of innocence over that drug business. Yes, *you* would. But then sex does have a way of making certain women blind to certain men. I'll bet you couldn't wait to get into bed with him once you'd found out the truth, could you?'

She looked quite ugly in her contempt. 'God! You make me sick, Ashleigh O'Neil. You probably only agreed to marry James so you could close your eyes every night and pretend he was Jake!'

'Have you heard enough, Leigh?' Jake said coldly, but placing a surprisingly warm arm around her by now shivering body.

'Y...yes,' she stammered, stunned by Nancy's vicious attack.

'Let's go, then.'

'You can't take James's car!' his mother screamed after them.

Jake whirled. 'Just try and stop me, Mother. You're damned lucky that you and your precious James are getting off this easily. I could have pulled the plug on his little scheme with a very loud pop today. But I didn't. One of the reasons I went through with that fiasco of a marriage was to save James's reputation, as well as your miserable social position in this town. But somehow I don't think you'll be quite so generous with *Ashleigh's* reputation, will you? I can hear you now, after we're gone...

'"You've no idea what happened on poor James's honeymoon,"' Jake mimicked in Nancy's best plum-in-the-mouth voice. '"Ashleigh ran into Jake again and you wouldn't believe it! The wretched creature ran off with him. The poor boy is just devastated. I don't think he'll ever marry again..."'

'Close, am I, Mother?' he taunted.

Nancy lifted her patrician nose. 'James is not really gay. He's been led astray, that's all, by a wicked, wicked man. I have to protect him till he's himself again.'

'You know what, Mother?' Jake said wearily. 'I actually agree with you. And who knows? Maybe, in time, he'll get rid of that corrupting creep and eventually meet a girl like my Leigh and fall in love.'

Suddenly Nancy's icy control cracked. 'Do you think so, Jake?' she choked out. 'Do you really?'

Both Ashleigh and Jake looked at each other in amazement when Nancy burst into tears, her slender, almost frail body racked with heart-rending sobs.

Ashleigh's soft womanly heart was moved, and she stepped forward to take the distressed woman in her arms. 'There, there, Nancy,' she soothed, hugging her and patting her on the back. 'James will be all right. Either way he's a good man, and I love him dearly, just as you do, just as his brother does. We all want to protect him from hurt, don't we, Jake?'

Jake looked at her and sighed. 'I guess so, but not at your expense, Leigh.'

'Then why don't the three of us go inside and think of some way out of this mess? Glenbrook is our home, Jake. We want the right to be able to come here occasionally and visit, without undue scandal and gossip.'

His eyes narrowed to stare at her. 'Come back, Leigh? That suggests leaving in the first place. Does that mean…you *are* going to come with me?'

If Ashleigh had ever had any doubt about her love for Jake it vanished at that moment. To see him looking at her like that. So hopeful…so tense…so vulnerable…

This was not the same arrogant young blood she'd once known. This was a sensitive human being, who'd been to hell and back and somehow survived. But not without a great deal of damage. He was so right when he said he needed her. She could see it in his strained face, and in the way he wasn't breathing while he waited for her answer.

'Of course, Jake,' she whispered, a lump in her throat. 'You were right all along. I love you. And I want to be your wife, wherever that takes me…'

They stared at each other over the bowed head of his weeping mother, and neither needed to say a thing. It was all there, in the intense relief in his eyes, and the glistening love in hers.

'I hope we can come up with a damned good solution for all this mess, then,' he said in an emotion-charged voice. 'Because I want everything to be right for you, my darling. You deserve it.'

Kate stared at all three of them across the large kitchen table. 'I still don't believe it!' she exclaimed. 'When the telephone rang in the middle of the night I was sure there'd been some terrible accident. I would never have dreamt...' She darted another wide-eyed glance Jake's way, then shook her head. 'I should have known,' she muttered under her breath. 'So damned masterful... Not like James at all...'

'You weren't the only one who was fooled,' Ashleigh said, throwing an accusing though indulgent look Jake's way.

'Really?' Kate speculated. 'When did you—er...?'

Her voice trailed away when Ashleigh looked daggers at her.

'Yes, well...best I don't ask that, I think. Just as well I moved out of home and into the small flat above my salon,' she went on blithely, 'or I'd have had to explain to my mother why you were dragging me out in the middle of the night of your wedding, Ashleigh. Come to think of it, why *have* you? I mean, I'm glad you told me the rather astonishing truth about everything, and I think Jake's switching with James is rather romantic in a weird sort of way, but what can I do to help?'

'I want you to make sure the whole town knows the truth. No, not about James,' she quickly amended, hearing the gasp of shock from Nancy, 'but about Jake's having taken his brother's place at the wedding. You can act as if the families and close friends were all in on it, but didn't say anything at the last moment for fear of causing an uproar among the more elderly guests. Relay all this confidentially to some selected customers of your salon, adding that James and I were already having doubts about our marriage and that when Jake arrived home for the wedding I realised he was still the man for me. It probably won't occur to anyone to question how we got a licence so quickly, but if they do just say we told the authorities a mistake was made with the names...'

When Kate looked totally perplexed James explained to her about how Jake was another form of John and that he and James actually had the same names, only reversed.

'Goodness!' she exclaimed. 'Then when the celebrant said John James at the ceremony he really meant it. It wasn't just a boo-boo?'

'No boo-boo,' Jake confirmed. 'I wasn't about to promise to love, honour and cherish my darling Leigh here in another man's name.'

Kate looked very impressed.

'Then after you've spread all that around, Kate,' Ashleigh continued, 'you'd better also add that James decided he was still in love with some girl he'd been seeing in Brisbane last year and was going off to try and win her back.'

'Goodness, Leigh, how inventive you've become over the years,' Jake said with some amusement in his voice.

'Not at all, Jake,' Kate denied drily. 'She's as disgustingly practical as always. Believe me, this is her idea of forging her own destiny.'

'Sounds good to me,' he grinned. 'As long as I'm in there somewhere, she can forge away all she likes.'

'Be quiet, the both of you,' Ashleigh reprimanded. 'I'm thinking... Yes, and it might not be a bad idea to also let drop some ''hush-hush'' news about how Jake was wrongly convicted all those years ago and that was the real reason why the Thai government eventually released him. No one will bother to check, and if you tell everyone it's supposed to be a secret it'll get around like wildfire.'

'I'll tell Mrs Brown. She has her hair done on Monday.' Kate's eyes glittered with relish at the task. 'Oh, and Maisie Harrison. She's coming in on Tuesday and has just been elected president of the local ladies' guild. Don't worry. There won't be a soul in town who won't know everything within a day or two.'

'Now, Nancy...' Ashleigh turned to the woman sitting next to her. Jake's mother was still very pale, though she had pulled herself together once she'd known Kate was on her way over. 'You'll have to ring my father in the morning and get him over here on a house call. Say you feel ill. That way, when you tell him the truth about James and Jake and everything, he won't be able to tell anyone because of his having to keep your confidence. I'll write a letter as well that you can give him, explaining my feelings for Jake and that I've gone off with him. I think he'll be understanding.'

Privately Ashleigh knew her father wouldn't be too broken up over his daughter's leaving Glenbrook, other than how he and his partner would be inconvenienced till Stuart joined the practice next year. In her letter she would suggest he hire a woman locum to fill in, warning him that if he didn't watch out a smart woman doctor would set up practice in Glenbrook and steal half his patients.

'But where will you and Jake go?' Kate asked.

Ashleigh looked at Jake. 'Darling? Where are we going?' she smiled at him, and when he smiled back an incredible sensation of bonding wrapped tentacles around her heart. He was so right. They did belong together. How could she ever have doubted it? Here in Glenbrook or out the back of Bourke or over in a small village in Thailand in an old grass hut. It didn't matter, as long as they were together.

'To Brisbane first, I think,' he said. 'I'll ring Rhys—he's staying at the Glenbrook Hotel. He'll drive us to Brisbane Airport, where we can see about booking tickets to Thailand. Have you got a current passport?'

'Yes.' Ashleigh tactfully declined mentioning that part of her honeymoon had been arranged for Hawaii. 'It's in my black handbag in the car.'

'Good, then there's no reason why we can't fly out to Bangkok straight away. My home is not far from there. Oh, and, by the way, it's far from a grass hut. It's quite grand, in fact. You see, Aunt Aggie left me all her money when she died, didn't you know?'

Ashleigh was taken aback. 'No,' she confessed. 'I didn't.'

'Neither did I!' Kate pronounced, sounding affronted that a piece of interesting gossip had somehow eluded her.

'I wrote to her when I got out of prison, telling her the whole truth. The old dear must have felt sorry for me and what I'd been through, and made me her heir. Six months later she was gone, and suddenly all my financial worries were over. Not only that, but I was also recently paid a packet for the film rights to a book of mine that's about to go on the stands in America. I'm loaded, my girl. Do you honestly think I'd expect you to rough it out in the wild somewhere? Not that I'm not flattered that you were prepared to.'

'Rhys told me that he was going to make a movie in Thailand,' Kate said with a frown. 'But I didn't make any connection with you, Jake.'

'Just as well,' Jake returned with feeling. 'As it is, I told Rhys not to talk about Thailand, but that man can't stop gabbling on about his damned movies.'

'You know he said if I ever wanted a job with his company as a hairdresser on set he'd be only too happy to oblige. You know what? I think I'll take him up on it.'

'What kind of book, Jake?' Ashleigh asked, a well of emotion filling her heart. He'd always said he'd be a great author one day. How proud of him she felt!

'A fictionalised version of my experiences in Thailand. Not all bad, either. It's a great country, you know, despite everything it put me through. Not that I can really blame the authorities. The man responsible for my imprisonment was damnably clever.'

'Yes, I'd like to know more about that,' his mother joined in. 'How *could* heroin get to be in your luggage without your knowing?'

If there was still a truculent note in her voice Jake was man enough to ignore it. He gave a nonchalant shrug. 'It was a simple yet clever ruse,' he explained. 'There was this fellow Australian named Doug, staying in the same hotel in Bangkok. He was always reading, great, thick tomes in hardback. He'd been wading through one on the day before our flight home, raving on about how great it was, even to showing me a particular passage he found very moving. I politely read it, not thinking much of it myself, but not saying so.'

Jake's laugh was rueful. 'Little did I know that this was just to reassure me it was a real book with real contents. When he complained the next day that he couldn't fit it into his luggage, and that he really wanted to read the rest when he got back to Australia, I let him stash it in mine; unbeknown to me the middle section was hollowed out and stuffed with heroin. Just enough, unfortunately, to upgrade my crime from possession to trafficking. Naturally, when I was picked up at the airport he conveniently disappeared, with my not even knowing his full name.'

'But didn't your lawyers try to trace him?' Ashleigh asked.

'They said there was little point, since I had no independent witness to any of this. It would just be my word against his.'

Nancy was beginning to look guilty. 'That still sounds

negligent to me,' she muttered. 'They should have tried, the same as your father and I should have tried to find better lawyers for you, Jake. I...I'm sorry, son. We...we let you down...'

'It's all right, Mother. We all make mistakes in life, and we all have expectations of people that cannot sometimes be met. I was a difficult, selfish, rebellious young man back then. I can see that now. But I have matured and mellowed, I hope, even to trying to understand and forgive James. He only did what he did where Leigh was concerned because he was trying to live up to other people's expectations of him. Tell him when you see him, Mother, that you will love him, no matter what he is or does. That's very important. If you don't there's no hope for him. No hope at all.'

Nancy was not about to concede she had failed her favourite son in any way whatsoever. She stiffened, then stood up, proud and straight. 'I have a very good relationship with James. We love and trust each other. He...he didn't tell me about his...problem, because he knew it was just a phase he was going through. I'm sure he'll be fine once I can get him away from that wicked man.' She turned to face Ashleigh. 'I will try to explain all this to your father in the morning. Leave your letter here, on the table, and I'll give it to him. But, for now, I...I must go to bed. I'm very, very tired.'

Ashleigh also got to her feet. 'I'll walk up with you, Nancy. Jake...perhaps you could ring Rhys while I'm gone.'

'Right away.'

The two women did not speak as they walked side by side up the stairs. They stopped outside Nancy's bedroom door. 'Don't worry about Jake and me, Nancy,' she said in parting. 'We'll be fine...'

Nancy gave her a rueful look. 'Oh, I can see that. You and Jake were somehow meant to be, Ashleigh. He was your destiny.'

'Maybe, Nancy. Maybe...'

Ashleigh turned away with an ironic expression on her face. Destiny had nothing to do with it, she still firmly believed. One made choices in life. Tonight she had *chosen* to spend the rest of her life with Jake.

She walked briskly along the corridor and turned into the bedroom at the top of the stairs, where she retrieved the locket from under the bed and the chain from the chest of drawers. Clutching it tightly in her hand, she made her way downstairs, where Jake was just hanging up the telephone in the foyer.

'Rhys is on his way,' he said, his eyes searching her face as she joined him. 'Are you sure, Leigh? I'm not rushing you, am I?'

'Of course you're rushing me,' she laughed. 'But no matter.' She moved into his arms and raised her face for him to kiss her.

He did so, gently and reverently. 'I really love you. You must know that. It's not just sex.'

'I know,' she admitted at last, and, taking his hand, pressed the locket back in it.

'What's this?'

'I'm giving you my heart again,' she said softly. 'But not on loan this time. This is for keeps.'

He stared down at the delicate locket and thought of all the long, lonely nights he had held it to his own heart and cried for the girl who'd once given it to him. Well, there would be no more lonely nights, no more despair. He would gather this lovely, loving woman to his heart and treasure her till his dying days.

'I'll give it to our first daughter,' he said in a thickened tone. 'And when she's old enough I'll tell her the story behind it.'

Ashleigh linked arms with him and they started walking slowly back to the kitchen, where Kate was sure to be waiting impatiently for them. 'How many children would you like, Jake?' she asked softly.

'Lots.'

'That's good. Because if I've done my sums right expect the first in about nine months' time.'

When she looked up at him, expecting a measure of shock, Jake was smiling wryly down at her.

'Jake Hargraves!' she gasped. 'You *knew* I might get pregnant tonight, didn't you?'

'Aye,' he agreed with mock contrition. 'That I did. James let the cat out of the bag when I—er—questioned him about how far things had gone between you two.'

'But why...I mean...why didn't you say something?'

'I thought I'd best keep an ace up my sleeve, in case you decided we weren't quite right for each other. I rather thought a wee babe might change your mind.'

'Why, you sneaky, rotten...'

'My God, you two aren't fighting already, are you?' Kate groaned from the kitchen doorway.

'Who? Us?' Jake scooped an arm around Ashleigh's waist and pulled her close to his side. 'Never!'

'Certainly not,' Ashleigh giggled, seeing the funny side of it.

Kate eyed them both suspiciously. 'I hope not. People make their own luck in life, isn't that what you always say, Ashleigh?'

'Oh, definitely.'

'In that case,' she rushed forward, an anxious look on her face, 'would you have a spare room for me in

Thailand if I came over for a while after I find a buyer for my salon? I think I'll take Rhys up on his offer.'

The front doorbell rang, and Jake stepped over to open it.

Rhys stood there, an equally anxious look on his face. 'All right, give me the bad news. She sent you packing once she found out, didn't she? I did tell you, Jake, this wasn't the way to handle it. Women don't like to be deceived, you know. They...'

He gaped into silence when Ashleigh walked forward and slipped a loving arm through Jake's. 'Now, Rhys, don't be so melodramatic. I'm not angry with Jake at all. I adore him and we're going to Thailand together to live and have babies while Jake writes and I doctor. We have only one further favour to ask of you.'

His mouth flapped open, but no words came out.

'Of both of you, actually,' she went on, her glance encompassing Kate as well. 'Would you two be our witnesses again when we really, truly get married, *legally* next time?'

'Well, of course,' Rhys agreed, still rather bemused by the turn of events.

'But only if you uphold all the traditions,' Kate inserted sternly. 'White dress and all the trimmings. I don't believe in any of those register office jobs.'

Ashleigh grinned. 'All right, Miss Tradition. But you'll have to come up with a different "something borrowed" for me. That locket just won't do any more. It's been "returned to sender".' And she looked lovingly up at Jake.

'Returned to...' Kate frowned. 'But I thought Nancy had... I mean... Ashleigh O'Neil!' she wailed. 'You've been keeping secrets from me!'

'I wonder why,' she laughed, and, smiling, went up on tiptoe to kiss the man she loved.

HARLEQUIN®

AN IMPORTANT MESSAGE FROM THE EDITORS OF HARLEQUIN®

Dear Reader,

Because you've chosen to read one of our fine romance novels, we'd like to say "thank you"! And, as a **special** way to thank you, we've selected <u>four more</u> of the <u>books</u> you love so well, **and** a beautiful Cherub Magnet to send you absolutely *FREE!*

Please enjoy them with our compliments...

Candy Lee

Editor,
Presents

P.S. And because we value our customers, we've attached something extra inside...

EDITOR'S
FREE
GIFT
SEAL
THANK YOU

PEEL OFF SEAL AND PLACE INSIDE

HOW TO VALIDATE
YOUR
EDITOR'S FREE GIFT
"THANK YOU"

1. Peel off gift seal from front cover. Place it in space provided at right. This automatically entitles you to receive four free books and a lovely Cherub Magnet.

2. Send back this card and you'll get brand-new Harlequin Presents® novels. These books have a cover price of $3.50 each, but they are yours to keep absolutely free.

3. There's no catch. You're under no obligation to buy anything. We charge nothing — ZERO — for your first shipment. And you don't have to make any minimum number of purchases — not even one!

4. The fact is thousands of readers enjoy receiving books by mail from the Harlequin Reader Service® . They like the convenience of home delivery...they like getting the best new novels BEFORE they're available in stores...and they love our discount prices!

5. We hope that after receiving your free books you'll want to remain a subscriber. But the choice is yours — to continue or cancel, anytime at all! So why not take us up on our invitation, with no risk of any kind. You'll be glad you did!

6. Don't forget to detach your FREE BOOKMARK. And remember...just for validating your Editor's Free Gift Offer, we'll send you FIVE MORE gifts, *ABSOLUTELY FREE!*

This charming refrigerator magnet looks like a little cherub, and it's a perfect size for holding notes and recipes. Best of all it's yours ABSOLUTELY FREE when you accept our NO-RISK offer!

THE EDITOR'S "THANK YOU"
FREE GIFTS INCLUDE:

▶ Four BRAND-NEW romance novels
▶ A beautiful Cherub Magnet

PLACE
FREE GIFT
SEAL
HERE

YES! I have placed my Editor's "thank you" seal in the space provided above. Please send me 4 free books and a lovely Cherub Magnet. I understand I am under no obligation to purchase any books, as explained on the back and on the opposite page.

106 CIH CCLA (U-H-P-09/97)

_____
NAME

_____
ADDRESS   APT.

_____
CITY   STATE   ZIP

Thank you!

THE HARLEQUIN READER SERVICE®: HERE'S HOW IT WORKS

Accepting free books places you under no obligation to buy anything. You may keep the books and gift and return the shipping statement marked "cancel". If you do not cancel, about a month later we will send you 6 additional novels, and bill you just $2.90 each plus 25¢ delivery per book and applicable sales tax, if any*. That's the complete price, and—compared to cover prices of $3.50 each—quite a bargain! You may cancel at any time, but if you choose to continue, every month we'll send you 6 more books, which you may either purchase at the discount price…or return to us and cancel your subscription.

*Terms and prices subject to change without notice. Sales tax applicable in N.Y.

SUSAN NAPIER

Vendetta

To my father, Ted Hedges, the Intrepid Traveller

CHAPTER ONE

THE time had come.

Ten years...

For ten years he had looked forward to this moment with a savage anticipation that had blotted out all lesser ambitions. He had forced himself to watch, to wait, to plan, to carry on with the rest of his life as if revenge had not become the pivot of his existence.

Of course, outside the waiting, the plotting, he had gone through all the right motions, maintaining the fiction of Christian forgiveness...smiling, talking, moving, interacting with those around him, accepting their praise for his achievements, cultivating their admiration and envy, consolidating his wealth. But none of it had had any meaning, any reality for him.

The admiration, the envy, the wealth were necessary only as a source of power. The power to see justice done. The power to punish...

He pressed his right hand on the hard, highly polished surface of his desk, watching the faint mist of heat from his skin bloom across the cool, dark surface between his splayed fingers. A heavy gold ring engraved with an entwined briar and snake on the flat shield flashed in the firelight, the only source of light in the coldly elegant room, as he turned his hand over and stared at the bold tracery of life-lines on his palm. They mocked him with their energy. He had had such grand hopes of life until *she* had come along and casually crushed them.

But now the long, bitter years of waiting were over. He finally had her exactly where he wanted her...in the palm of his powerful hand. And the timing was perfect. She thought that she was safe. She thought that she had got away with it, that everyone had forgotten her crime. Soon, very soon, she would learn differently. There was no statute of limitations on murder.

He curled his fingers inward to form a brutal fist. All he had to do now was close the trap and watch her futile struggles to free herself. She would probably weep and cry innocence, or bluster and threaten, or, better still, cringe and beg for his entertainment. Then he would strip away her pride and her self-respect and stand witness to the death, one by one, of all her hopes and dreams. It was an image that he treasured in the depths of his embittered soul.

He picked up the squat crystal glass next to his hand and took a long swallow of potent, twelve-year-old Scotch. The raw, smoky bite at the back of his throat was pleasurable, but it was no match for the intoxicating taste of revenge that was flooding his senses. For the first time in a decade, he felt almost whole again.

The time had come...

CHAPTER TWO

VIVIAN took the last two steps in one grateful stride and then paused for breath, forcing herself to look back down the narrow staircase that was chipped out of the rocky face of the cliff.

In spite of the fact it was a cold and blustery day, typical of New Zealand's autumn, sweat was trickling down her torso inside her cream blouse and her palm had felt appallingly slippery on the single, stout wooden rail that had been the only barrier between her and the rock-strewn, sea-green oblivion below.

She shuddered faintly as she watched the two men far below, unloading the cargo from the hold of the squat little ferry-boat.

Reaction hit and Vivian swallowed, her dry mouth suddenly thick with moisture. Her legs felt like jelly and she swayed, fighting the urge to sink weakly to the ground.

She pressed a hand to her abdomen, trying to control the unpleasant churning feeling as she turned away and followed the sharply rising, stony path up through the low, scrubby trees. She had to get a grip on herself before she reached her destination. She smoothed down her neat dark green skirt and adjusted the matching blazer as she went, nervously switching the soft-sided leather satchel from one sweaty hand to the other as she tried to calm herself by projecting a mental aura of professionalism.

She had a reputation to uphold. She was here as a rep-

resentative of Marvel-Mitchell Realties to close a vital
property deal. A lot was depending on her. It wasn't just
the money, but the future happiness of people that she
loved that was at stake.

It hadn't helped that what she had been told was a
forty-minute journey from the north-east coast of the
Coromandel Peninsula to the island had actually taken
over an hour and a half in very choppy seas. After a
rushed three-hour drive from Auckland last evening, and
an anxious, wakeful night in an uncomfortable motel bed,
her close encounter with the Pacific Ocean had not been
pleasant.

Since her destination was the private island of a mil-
lionaire, Vivian had naïvely expected a luxury launch or
hydrofoil to be her mode of transport, not the ugly old
tub that she had been directed to at Port Charles. She had
also expected the island to be a lush private sanctuary,
with beautiful white-sand beaches and flourishing vege-
tation, rather than a wind-swept, surf-lashed rock in the
middle of nowhere. Although the name should have given
her a clue, she thought wryly.

Nowhere. She had thought it quaint; now she realised
it had been highly descriptive!

What kind of man would drag someone out all this way
to conclude a business deal that would have been better,
and more safely handled in a city office? Unfortunately,
she thought she knew exactly: a man bent on causing
trouble. A machiavellian man who would not be appeased
by an easy victory. If she was to thwart any of his aims
she would have to play his game first.

Vivian came through a small, wind-mutilated grove of
low-growing trees and halted, her mouth falling open in
shock.

Across a small ridge, perched on a flat tongue of land

at the end of a rocky promontory, was a lighthouse. If she hadn't been so busy hanging miserably over the rail of the boat, wondering whether to cast up her rushed motel breakfast into the sea, she would have seen the tall white tower as they approached the island.

She lifted bleak eyes from the wide concrete base, up, up past the vertical line of four tiny windows to stare at the open balcony just below the diamond-shaped glass panes that housed the light. How many stairs to get to the top of *that*?

Her appalled gaze sank back down again and settled with overpowering relief on the low, white-painted concrete building that adjoined the towering structure. A keeper's cottage.

She got a grip on herself. No need to let your imagination run wild, Vivian. All New Zealand lighthouses were now automated. It might even have been decommissioned. She had no business with lighthouses. It was the man in the nice, ordinary, *low* building beside it that she had come to see!

The narrow pathway across the short ridge was fenced on both sides with white pickets, offering her at least a notion of security as the wind swept up one side of the steep, rocky face and wrenched at her hair and clothes with berserk glee. She touched each picket with her free hand as she passed, counting to take her mind off what lay at either side, aware that her neat bun was unravelling more with every step.

By the time she reached the stout, weathered timber door, she was resigned to looking like a freak. A quick glance at her reflection in the curtained window beside the door confirmed the worst. Her shoulder-length hair, inclined to be wild and woolly at the best of times, was making the most of its partial freedom in the moisture-laden air, and there was no time to try and torture the tight ginger curls back into businesslike obedience. Hurriedly Vivian pulled out the few remaining pins. Now, instead of resembling a lop-sided hedgehog, she merely looked like a frightened lion.

She took a deep breath, straightened the side-seams of her skirt, and knocked loudly.

After several moments she knocked again, then again. Finally she tried the door-handle and found to her surprise that it opened easily. She tentatively edged across the threshold.

'Hello, is anybody there? Mr Rose? Mr Rose!' The door closed behind her with a weighty clunk, sounding unpleasantly like the door to a cell.

She walked warily down the short narrow hall and into a large room, sparsely furnished in everything except books—walls of them.

A long, well-used, brown leather couch was drawn up in front of a coal-blackened fireplace and there was a big roll-top desk and chair beside a window overlooking the sea. Another small port-hole window among the books showed the smooth white rise of the adjoining lighthouse tower. There were a few rugs on the polished hardwood floor and a large, smooth-sided antique chest that obviously doubled as a coffee-table, but there were no ornaments or plants, paintings or photographs. Nothing that betrayed the excessive wealth of the owner. Nothing but the books to give the room character…and a rather daunting one at that, thought Vivian, eyeing some of the esoteric titles.

Like the adjacent lighthouse, the house was obviously designed to withstand the constant buffeting of seastorms, the interior walls made of the same thick, roughcast cement as the outer shell. She wondered nervously whether perhaps it was also designed to endure buffetings from within. The mysterious and formerly benignly eccentric Mr Rose, with whom Marvel-Mitchell Realties had dealt quietly and successfully for years via lawyer, letter and fax, was shaping up to be a chillingly ruthless manipulator. She didn't doubt for one minute that this wait was designed to make her sweat.

Unless he had never intended to turn up at all.

Vivian shivered. She put her briefcase down by the desk and began to pace, trying to burn off her increasing tension. There were no clocks in the room and she checked her watch frequently as ten minutes ticked slowly past. The captain had said the boat would be leaving again in an hour. If Mr Rose hadn't arrived by then she would simply leave.

To pass the time, she re-applied her lipstick and brushed her hair, cursing herself for not tucking extra hairpins into her bag, when suddenly her restless thoughts were drowned out by a loud, rhythmic beating that seemed to vibrate through the walls. Vivian turned towards the window to see a sleek white helicopter descending towards a flat circle of tussock just below the cottage.

She felt her temper fizzle bracingly as the craft settled to rest and the door opened and two men got out, heads ducked low as they battled the whirlwind created by the slowing blades.

Nicholas Rose had a helicopter! Instead of her spending an eternity on a heaving boat, he could have had her *flown* out to the island in minutes! For that matter, he could probably have got to Auckland and back in the time it had taken her to cross the angry patch of water.

She watched as the first passenger, a huge, blond bear of a man in jeans and a sheepskin jacket, stood back and respectfully allowed the man in the dark blue suit to pass him.

Vivian studied the man whom she had travelled all this way to see. Even bowed over, he was tall, and he looked lean and fit, with dark hair and a face that, as he glanced up towards the house, was hard and rugged. He grinned at something that was said behind him and her heart leapt with hope as the grimness dropped away from him and he looked comfortingly sane and civilised. The other one, the beefy blond who shadowed his footsteps with a cat-like alertness, had bodyguard written all over him. They disappeared around the back of the cottage. Vivian was facing the door, her hands clasped nervously behind her, when finally, after another agonised age, it opened.

She bit off a frustrated groan when the jeans-clad figure stepped into the room. Another carefully orchestrated delay, no doubt designed to undermine further her dwindling confidence. Or was the bodyguard here to check her for concealed weapons?

Her eyes darted to his face and the breath caught with a shock in her throat. There was a black patch over his left eye, a thin scar running vertically from his hairline to the top of the concealing inverted triangle and from beneath it down over his high cheekbone to the slanting plane of his cheek. The other eye was light brown, and Vivian's gaze hastily skidded down, afraid he would think she was staring.

His mouth was thin and his face uncompromisingly square and deeply tanned, his thick, straight hair—wheat-gold at the ends and several shades darker at the roots—raked carelessly back from the scarred forehead by fingers and the wind, the shaggy ends brushing the upturned collar of his jacket. Darker gold glinted on the angles of the jutting jaw as his head shifted, revealing at least a day's growth of beard. Even with the eye-patch and the scar he was good-looking, in a reckless, lived-in, don't-give-a-damn kind of way.

Without speaking, he shouldered out of the hip-length jacket and she could see that its bulk had given her a deceptive impression of the man. He wasn't really the behemoth he had first appeared. Although his wine-red roll-necked sweater moulded a fairly impressive pair of shoulders, and was stretched to accommodate a deep chest, his body narrowed to a lean waist and hips that indicated not an ounce of unnecessary fat. His legs were very long, the muscles of his thighs thick enough to strain the faded denim. His hands, as he tossed the discarded jacket effortlessly halfway across the room to land over the back of the couch, were strong and weathered. Big, capable hands. Capable of hurting...or healing, she thought, startled at the unlikely notion that came floating up through her sluggish brain.

He leaned back against the door, snicking it closed with a shift of his weight, bending his knee to brace the sole of a scuffed leather boot on the wood behind him, crossing his arms over his chest. Vivian forced her gaze to rise again, to discover that she wasn't the only person who appeared to be shocked into a momentary trance. The single, brown eye was unblinkingly studying her, seemingly transfixed by the vivid aureole of hair surrounding her tense face.

Another man with conventional ideas about feminine beauty! She knew her own myriad imperfections well enough; she didn't need his startled stare to remind her. As if the scalding brightness of her hair wasn't enough, her green eyes had the garish brilliance of cheap glass, hardly muted by the lenses of her round spectacles, and a mass of ginger freckles almost blotted out her creamy skin.

Vivian's left hand lifted to smooth down the springy ginger mane around her shoulders, and she smiled tentatively at him, flushing when he didn't respond. A small freckled pleat appeared just above the gold wire bridge of her glasses, and she adjusted them unnecessarily on her straight nose, giving him the 'tough' look that she had practised in the motel mirror the previous night.

'Well, well, well...the Marvel-lous Miss Mitchell, I presume?'

His voice was like silk drawn over rough gravel, sarcastically smooth with a rustling hint of hard, underlying crunch.

A voice used to giving orders. To being obeyed. No polite deference or preening arrogance here. Just utter authority.

Vivian clenched her hands behind her back as the unpalatable truth burst upon her.

She would have far preferred to deal with the civilised Suit! A Suit might be persuaded to sacrifice a small victory for an immediate, larger gain.

This man looked too unconventional, too raw-edged, too primitive ever to have heard of the words 'negotiated surrender'. He looked like a man who enjoyed a fight—and had had plenty of them.

Looking defeat in the face, Vivian knew there was no going back. She *had* to try and beat him at his own game. But no one said she had to play it solely by his rules.

CHAPTER THREE

'THE elusive Mr Rose, I presume?' Vivian echoed his mocking drawl, hoping that she sounded a lot more in control of herself than she felt.

There was a small, challenging silence. He inclined his head, still studying her with the arrested fascination of a scientist confronting a new form of life.

Vivian smoothed her hands nervously down the side-seams of her skirt, and to her horror her fingers encountered the crumpled tail of her blouse trailing from beneath the back of her unbuttoned jacket. Somehow it must have worked free on that nerve-racking climb. Trying to maintain her dignity, she continued to meet his dissecting stare coolly, while surreptitiously tucking her blouse back into the waistband of her skirt.

He noticed, of course, and a curious flicker lightened his expression before it settled back into brooding aggression.

'So...do we now blithely proceed from our mutual presumptions, or do we observe strict propriety and introduce ourselves properly?'

His murmur was rife with hidden meanings, and Vivian hesitated, wondering whether she was reading her own guilt into his words.

'Uh—well, I think we know who we are...' She closed her eyes briefly, cursing herself for her faltering of courage at the critical moment.

When she opened them again, he was metaphorically crouched in waiting.

'I think, therefore I am?' he said softly. 'Very profound, my dear, but I'm sure Descartes intended his philosophy to be applied to something more meaningful than social introductions. However, far be it from me to contradict a lady, particularly such a highly qualified one as yourself. So, we have an agreement that I'm Nicholas Rose of Nowhere and you are Miss Mitchell of Marvel-Mitchell Realties. Welcome to my world, Miss Mitchell.'

He kicked himself away from the door and walked swiftly towards her, hand outstretched. Without looking down, she was aware that he limped. She was also aware of the savage pride in the single, glittering eye which effortlessly dominated her attention. It seemed to flame with a strange inner light, until the almond-brown iris was shot with blazing spears of gold as he came to a stop in front of her, closer than was comfortable or courteous, towering over her by at least six inches as he insolently invaded her personal space.

She accepted his proffered hand with a wariness that proved wise when the strength of his grip turned out to be even greater than she had anticipated. His hand wrapped almost completely around hers, trapping it as he extended the moment of contact beyond politeness into the realm of pure intimidation.

The calluses on his palm as he eased the pressure created a friction against her softer skin which felt disturbingly familiar. It was like the faint warning buzz she had experienced when touching a faulty electrical socket. Indeed, the very air around him seemed to crackle and carry a whiff of burning. It was as if there was a huge energy source humming inside him, barely restrained by flesh and blood.

He released her slightly maimed fingers, the gold flecks in his eye glowing with a strange satisfaction as she stayed stubbornly where she was, lifting her firm chin, refusing to be daunted by his superior size and strength, or by the unsettling reciprocal hum in her own bones.

Surprisingly, he was first to disengage from the silent duel, turning away to sling himself down in the chair at the desk, stretching his long legs out in front of him. He didn't offer her a seat, just leaned back and regarded her in a way that seemed indefinably possessive. Vivian's blood tingled in her cheeks and she adjusted her spectacles again.

His thin mouth curved cruelly. 'Shall we proceed to the business in hand, then, Miss Mitchell? I take it you followed all the instructions in the fax?'

She thought of the tense drive down, the nerve-racking hours alone in the motel, the wallowing boat...and his helicopter. She set her teeth and nodded.

'Truly a Marvel—an obedient woman,' he punned goadingly, and Vivian's flush deepened with the effort of controlling her temper. 'And, knowing that your company's successful purchase of my land depends on your pandering to my every annoying little whim, of course you followed those instructions *to the letter*, did you not, Miss Mitchell?'

This time she wasn't going to chicken out. She squared her shoulders. 'No. That is, not exactly—'

'Not *exactly*? You do surprise me, Miss Marvel-lous.'

Nerves slipped their leash. 'Will you stop calling me that?'

'Perhaps I should call you Miss Marmalade instead. That would be a more descriptive nickname—your hair being the colour it is... That wouldn't offend you, would it? After all, what's in a name? "That which we call a rose by any other name would smell as sweet"...'

His frivolity was definitely a trap, the quotation from *Romeo and Juliet* containing a baited message that Vivian could not afford to acknowledge without betraying her tiny but infinitely precious advantage.

'As a matter of fact, there's an awful *lot* in a name,' she said, ignoring the lure. 'Mine, for example, is *Vivian* Mitchell—'

Instead of leaping to his feet in justifiable outrage, he rocked his chair on to its back legs with his booted heels, his expression one of veiled malice as he interrupted her confession. 'Vivian. Mmm, yes, you're right,' he mused, in that low, gratingly attractive voice. 'Vivian... It does have a certain aptness to your colouring, a kind of phonetic and visual rhythm to it...razor-sharp edges springing up around singing vowels. I do have your permission to call you Vivian, don't I, Miss Mitchell?'

'Yes, of course,' she bit off, his feigned innocence making her feel like a mouse between the paws of a lion. 'But you requested that *Janna* Mitchell bring you the documents and co-sign the settlement. Unfortunately my sister couldn't come, so I brought them instead. Otherwise, everything is exactly as you asked...'

'She couldn't come?' he asked mildly. 'Why not?'

Having expected a savage explosion of that banked energy, Vivian was once more disconcerted by his apparent serenity.

She moistened her lower lip nervously, unconsciously emphasising its fullness. 'She has flu.'

Janna was also sick with guilt and remorse, and the combination had made her pathetically easy to deceive. As far as her sister or anyone else knew, Vivian's prime motive for taking her place on this trip was her desperate desire to get away from everyone for a while.

'Convenient.'

She winced at the flick of the whip. Not so serene, after all.

'Not for her. Janna hates being ill.' Her younger sister was ambitious. As a newly qualified lawyer, working in Marvel-Mitchell Realties' legal department, she had a rosy future ahead of her, one that Vivian intended to protect.

'Messes up those gorgeous ice-blonde looks, I suppose,' he said, casting a sardonic look at her wild ginger mane.

Vivian froze.

'You knew,' she whispered, feeling momentarily faint. Thank God the masquerade had only been intended to get her inside the door.

'The moment I saw you.'

'But you've never met Janna—or anyone from Marvel-Mitchell,' she said hollowly. 'Until now you've always insisted on dealing through an intermediary—'

'So you decided to be honest, in spite of the fact I might be none the wiser for the deception. I'm impressed. Or was I supposed to be?' he added cynically. 'Are you always so honest, I wonder?'

'I try to be.' Her tartness reproved his cynicism.

'A neat piece of sophistry. You try but you don't necessarily always succeed, mmm?' His voice hardened. 'You can't have been so naïve as to think I wouldn't investigate the people I do business with? I'm not a fool.'

'I never thought you were.' But she had seriously underestimated his thoroughness.

'I'm sure that Marvel, too, conducted its own investigations into my integrity...?'

It was a question rather than a comment, and Vivian answered it as such.

'Other than maintaining a current credit check, Peter felt there was no need, since we've been buying and selling properties on your behalf for several years without any problems,' she replied curtly. 'In spite of never having met you, Peter considers you a trusted ally. So your personal integrity was naturally taken for granted, Mr Rose.' Her green eyes were wide and innocent as she made the final, pointed statement.

'Call me Nick, Vivian.' His reaction was equal bland innocence. 'Of course, one man's integrity is another man's poison. I don't do business with cheats and liars.'

'Very wise,' she agreed distractedly, unnerved by his mention of poison. Was that supposed to be significant?

'Are you patronising me, Miss Mitchell?' he asked silkily, planting his feet back on the floor and leaning his torso threateningly towards her.

She was jolted out of her unsettling ruminations. 'I prefer to think of it as pandering to your every annoying little whim,' she said sweetly.

There was another small, dangerous silence. He seemed to specialise in them.

He rose, unfolding himself to his full height with sinister slowness.

'Brave, aren't you?' he murmured.

The thin, menacing smile and the burning gold splinters in his eye told her it was not a compliment. 'So... Instead of the lawyer I requested, Marvel-Mitchell Realties sends me a mere receptionist. A suspicious man might take that as an insult...'

'But then, from your investigations you must know I'm not *just* a receptionist,' Vivian defended herself. 'I'm also Peter Marvel's secretary/PA, and for the last eighteen months a full financial partner in the firm. I'm fully authorised to sign cheques and contracts on behalf of Marvel-Mitchell Realties.'

Not that she ever had. Up until now she had been quite happy to be Peter's sleeping partner—well, lightly dozing at any rate. She enjoyed her work and hadn't looked on the investment of her unexpected inheritance in Peter's firm as an excuse to throw her weight around the office, but rather as an investment in their shared future...

Brooding on that sadly faded dream, she didn't notice him moving until a large hand was suddenly in front of her face. For an awful moment she thought his repressed hostility had finally erupted, but instead of the impact of his palm against her cheek, she felt him pull off her spectacles so that his image immediately dissolved into an indistinct blur.

'Oh, please...' She snatched vaguely, but he was too quick for her.

'Salt build-up from all that sea-spray on the boat trip,' he said blandly, retreating out of her reach. She squinted to see him produce a white square from his pocket and carefully rub the lenses with it. 'They need a good clean.'

He held them up to the light and inspected them before breathing on the glass and polishing some more. 'Pretty strong lenses. You must be extremely short-sighted.'

'I am,' she admitted truculently. She could have pointed out with brutal honesty that he had a few glaring imperfections of his own, but she was too soft-hearted for her own good—everyone said so. Even Peter, who was supposed to be madly in love with her, had always been exasperated by her ability to empathise with the opposing point of view in an argument.

'You must be rather helpless without them.'

Was that a hint of gloating in his voice? She squinted harder. 'Not helpless, just short-sighted,' she said flatly.

Unexpectedly he laughed. It was a disturbingly rich sound, unflavoured by bitterness. 'How long have you worn them?'

'Since I was thirteen.'

And never had she been more grateful, for once there were spectacles firmly perched on her nose she found the boys less inclined to stare endlessly at her ever-burgeoning breasts. From a potential sex-pot she had become an egg-head, and even though her marks had been barely average she had managed to cling to the image until the other girls in her class had also started acquiring ogle-worthy figures.

'May I have them back, please?' she asked the blurry male outline, holding out her hand.

There was a pause. All he had to do was clench those strong fingers and the fragile frames would be crushed, leaving her more vulnerable than ever.

'Of course.'

Instead of handing them to her, he replaced them himself, taking his time as he set them straight across the bridge of her nose, his face jumping back into disturbingly sharp focus, a close-up study in concentration as he tucked the ear-pieces carefully into place, his rough finger-pads sliding around on the ultra-sensitive skin behind her ears for long enough to make her shiver.

'Th-thank you,' she said reluctantly, edging back.

He followed her, his fingers still cradling the sides of her skull. 'You have very speaking eyes.' God, she hoped not! She blinked to clear her gaze of all expression and shuddered again at the intensity of his inspection. What was he searching for?

'Are you cold?'

'No.' To her dismay it came out as a breathy squeak.

His hands dropped to her taut shoulders, then lightly drifted down the outsides of her arms to her tense fists.

'You must be, after being out in that draughty old boat,' he contradicted. 'Your hands are as cold as ice and you're trembling. You need some food inside you to warm you up.'

She cleared her throat. 'I assure you, I'm perfectly warm,' she said, pulling her hands away. 'And I'm not hungry.'

'Your stomach still feeling the effects of the trip?' he murmured with annoying perception, his dark brown eyebrows lifted, the one above the eye-patch made raggedly uneven by the indent of the scar. 'It's a mistake to think the ride back will be easier on an empty stomach. You'll feel much better with something inside you.'

Like you? The wayward thought popped into her head and Vivian went scarlet.

He stilled, looking curiously at her bright face and the horrified green eyes that danced away from his in guilty confusion. What in the world was the matter with her?

His eyebrows settled back down and his eyelid drooped, disguising his expression as he took her silence as assent. 'Good, then you'll join me for lunch...'

'Thank you, but the boat leaves again in—' Vivian looked at her watch '—twenty minutes, and I still have to get back down to the wharf—'

'The captain won't leave until he's checked with me first.' He effortlessly cut the ground from under her feet.

'I'm really not hungry—'

'And if I said that I hadn't eaten since lunch yesterday and was far too ravenous to concentrate on anything but feeding my appetite?'

Your appetite for what? thought Vivian as she silently

weighed up her options…which proved to be extremely limited.

'I'd say *bon appétit*,' she sighed. Maybe he'd be easier to handle on a full stomach.

'On the principle that it's better I take bites out of food than out of you?' he guessed wolfishly, coming a little too close to her earlier, forbidden meanderings.

'Something like that,' she said primly.

'While I arrange something suitably light for you and filling for me, why don't you get those papers out so I can look them over?'

Looking them over was a long way from signing, but Vivian hastened to do as he instructed while he was gone. He had shut the door behind him, and opened it so quietly on his return that she wasn't aware of him until he loomed over her at the desk. The first she knew of him was the hot, predatory breath on the back of her neck.

'You move very quietly—' she began, in breathless protest at his consistent ability to surprise her.

'For a cripple?' he finished with biting swiftness.

'That wasn't what I was going to say!' she protested, sensing that sympathy was the last thing he would ever want from her.

'You were going to use a more diplomatic term, perhaps?' he sneered. 'Disabled? Physically challenged?'

She was suddenly blindly furious with him. How dared he think that she would be so callous, let alone so stupid, as to taunt him, no matter what the provocation!

'You move quietly for such a *big* man is what I was going to say before you rudely interrupted,' she snapped. 'And an over-sensitive one, too, I might add. *I* didn't leap down *your* throat when you drew attention to the fact I was blind as a bat, did I? And I have two supposedly undamaged legs and yet I never seem to be able to coordinate them properly. I dreamed of being a ballerina when I was a girl...' She trailed off wistfully, suddenly remembering who it was she was confiding in.

'A ballerina?' He looked at her incredulously, his sceptical eye running over her five-feet-ten frame and the generous curves that rumpled the professional smoothness of her suit.

'It was just a childish thing,' she said dismissively, inexplicably hurt by his barely concealed amusement.

He tilted his head. 'So you dreamed of becoming a perfect secretary instead?'

'I wasn't qualified for much else,' she said coldly. Academically she had been a dud, but she was responsible and willing and got on well with people, her final-year form-teacher had kindly pointed out to her concerned parents, and weren't those things far more important in attaining happiness in the wider world than the mere possession of a brilliant brain?

Of course some people—like Janna and their younger brother, Luke, who was a musical prodigy; and her mother and father, an artist and a mathematician respectively—managed to have it all...good looks included. Not that her family ever consciously made her feel inadequate. Quite the reverse—they sometimes went overboard in their efforts to convince her that she belonged, that she was the much-loved special one of the family. The Chosen One—because she had been adopted as a toddler, and had proved the unexpected catalyst for the rapid arrival of a natural daughter and then a son.

'No other thwarted ambitions?'

'No.' She didn't doubt he would laugh like a drain if she told him that her greatest desire was to be a wife and mother. It was her one outstanding talent: loving people—

even when they made it very difficult for her. Sometimes almost impossible.

She looked down at the documents on the desk, concentrating on squaring them off neatly, aware of a nasty blurring of her eyesight that had nothing to do with foggy glasses.

The papers were suddenly snatched out of her fingers. 'This is what you want *me* to sign?'

'Mmm?' Distracted by her thoughts, she took no notice of the faint emphasis. 'Oh, yes.' She pulled herself together, certain that her ugly suspicions were correct and that he was now going to announce dramatically that he had no intention of doing so.

Four months ago, when Nicholas Rose had signed a conditional agreement to sell his Auckland property, his lawyer had cited tax reasons for his client wishing to retain legal title until the end of April. Peter had been happy with the extended settlement date, for it had given him time to chase up the other parcels of land that had been part of the lucrative contract Marvel-Mitchell had entered into with a commercial property development company. Nicholas's property had been the most critical, being a corner lot at the front of the planned shopping mall development, providing the only street access to the larger site. With that in his pocket, Peter had felt free to bid up on one or two other lots, whose owners had demanded much more than current market price.

Then Nicholas Rose had suddenly cancelled his appointment to sign the settlement in Auckland, citing a clause in the conditional agreement that gave the vendor the right to choose the time and place, and Janna had got sick, and Vivian had tried to be helpful and discovered two appalling truths: one, that Nicholas Rose was potentially an implacable enemy, and two, that her cosy dream of love and babies with Peter was shattered beyond redemption.

For long minutes there was no sound but the quiet swish of paper turning, and Vivian's heart thundered in her ears as she waited for her enemy to reveal himself.

'Where do I sign?' He flicked cursorily back through the pages. 'Here? Here? And here?'

'Uh...yes.' He bent and she watched disbelievingly as he uncapped a fountain pen and scrawled his initials in the right places, ending with a full, flourishing signature. The solid gold band on his ring-finger caught her eye as his hand paused, and she stared at the etching of snake and rose, the same crest that she had seen on the letterhead in his lawyer's office.

'Now you.'

She numbly took his place as he stood aside. The shaft of the expensive pen was heavy and smooth, warm from his touch, and she was so nervous that she left a large blob after her name. He blotted it without comment.

'We'll need this properly witnessed, won't we?'

He didn't wait for an answer but went to the door and bellowed for 'Frank'.

The man in the dark suit came in. He gave Vivian a single, hostile, sharply assessing look, then took the proffered pen and co-signed the document with a tight-lipped frown.

'Satisfied?' he asked gratingly as he straightened up, throwing the pen down on to the desk.

'Thank you, Frank.'

Frank grunted.

'Lunch ready?' Nicholas Rose asked, seemingly undismayed by his employee's surly air of disapproval.

'In the kitchen. Just as you ordered, *sir*. Just don't expect me to serve it!'

'We'll serve ourselves.' He turned to Vivian, who was watching the by-play with slightly dazed green eyes, still stunned by the inexplicable reprieve. Could she have been wrong about him, after all? 'Frank heats up a mean soup. Frank is my right-hand man, by the way. Frank, this is Vivian.'

Another grunt and a bare acknowledgement.

'I think Vivian has something to give you before you go, Frank.'

'I do?' She looked at them both blankly.

'The money, Vivian,' Nicholas reminded her helpfully. 'If you haven't brought the cash and the bank-cheque, then this contract of sale isn't worth the paper it's written on.'

'Oh!' She blushed. How unprofessional. She was surprised he hadn't asked to see the money earlier. 'Oh, yes, of course. It's right here.'

She unfastened a locked compartment of her satchel, drawing out the thousand-dollar bundle of notes from a cloth bank-bag, and the crisp slip of paper that made up the balance. She was about to put them down on the desk when she hesitated, eyeing the settlement papers still splayed out in front of him, her fears blossoming anew. Her colour drained away as she nibbled her lip.

With a sardonic look, Nicholas Rose silently gathered up the papers and handed them to her. She tucked them hastily into the satchel before she gave him the bundles. She couldn't quite hide her relief at getting rid of the oppressive responsibility and was chagrined when he tossed the money casually to Frank, who stuffed it in his suit pockets and stumped out, muttering something about the pilot.

'This is all very unorthodox,' she said disapprovingly.

'I'm a very unorthodox man.' If that was a warning, it

had come far too late to be of any protection. 'Did it make you nervous travelling with such a large sum of cash?'

She thought of her sweaty drive and the almost sleepless night in the motel with a chair propped under the doorknob. 'Very.'

'Poor Vivian, no wonder you look so pale and tense.' He casually brushed her cheek with his thumb and she nearly went through the roof at the bolt of electricity that sizzled her senses.

They looked at each other, startled. His gaze dropped to her soft naked mouth, open in shock, then to the sliver of thickly freckled skin revealed by the modest cleavage of her blouse and the faint suggestion of lace hinted at by the trembling rise and fall of her lush breasts against the cream silk. In that single, brief glance he stripped her naked and possessed her.

'Come into the kitchen,' he said quietly. 'I know just what to give you to relax.'

He ushered her before him and she moved awkwardly, shaken by the most profoundly erotic experience of her life. And yet he had scarcely touched her! She felt confused, fearful and yet achingly alive, aware as never before of the feminine sway of her full hips and the brush of her thighs beneath her skirt. Her spine tingled in delicious terror. Was he stroking her again with that spiky look of hunger? Imagining how she would look moving in front of him without her clothes? She blushed in the dimness of the hall and chastised herself for her dangerous fantasies. Either it was all in her own mind, or Nicholas Rose had decided to set her up for a very personal form of humiliation. He couldn't possibly be genuinely attracted to her, not a man who, despite his physical flaws, possessed a raw magnetism that probably gave him his pick of beautiful women, not a man who showed every sign of being bent on vengeance.

The kitchen was small and compact and clearly the preserve of someone who enjoyed cooking. The bench-top was wooden, slicked with the patina of age, in contrast to the microwave and modern appliances, and in the small dining-alcove was a well-scrubbed kauri table and three chairs. Evidently Nowhere Island was not normally used for business entertaining.

The table was set with rush place-mats and solid silver cutlery, and the steaming bowl of thick, creamy, fragrant soup that was set before her made Vivian's tense stomach-muscles uncoil. There were bread rolls, too, which Nicholas got from the microwave, cursing as he burnt his fingers on the hot crusts.

The relaxant turned out to be a glass of champagne. And not just any old bubbly, but Dom Perignon. Vivian watched as he deftly opened the wickedly expensive bottle over her murmured protests that wine in the middle of the day made her sleepy, and turned his back to pour it into two narrow, cut-crystal flutes he had set on the bench.

Vivian drank some more soup, and when she was handed the chilled flute with a charming flourish accepted it fatalistically. What would be would doubtless be, whether she drank it or not.

'Have you ever tasted Dom Perignon before?' he asked, seating himself again, and this time applying himself to his soup with an appetite that definitely wasn't feigned.

'Why, yes, I have it every morning for breakfast, poured on my cornflakes,' she said drily.

'You must be a lively breakfast companion...albeit a more expensive one than most men could hope to afford,' he said, with a provocative smile that was calculated to distract.

But not you. It was on the tip of her tongue to say it, but she manfully refrained. 'I pay my own way.'

His eyes dropped to her hand, nervously tracing the grain of the table, and the smile was congealed.

'Yes, that's right, you do, don't you. Even to the extent of bank-rolling your fiancé's grand property schemes. I suppose you could say he gained a sleeping partner in more than one sense of the word...'

As she gasped in outrage, he lunged forward and trapped her left hand flat on the table-top, his palm pressing the winking diamond ring painfully into her finger.

'You've been working for him since you left school, haven't you? What took him so long to realise you were the woman of his dreams? It was around about the time you got that little windfall, wasn't it? Did he make it a condition of his proposal that you invest your inheritance in his business, or did you do it all for love?'

'How dare you imply it had anything to do with money?' she said fiercely, fighting the sudden urge to burst into pathetic tears and throw herself on his mercy. 'Peter asked me to marry him before he ever knew about the trust!' The release, on her twenty-third birthday, of funds from a trust set up by her natural parents had been a surprise to everyone, including her adoptive parents, who had refused to accept a cent of it. It was for Vivian to use how she wished, they had said—so she had.

'The wedding's this Saturday isn't it? Your twenty-fifth birthday?'

Her eyes lowered, her hand curling into a white-knuckled fist as she pulled it violently from under his and thrust it down into her lap. His investigations must have been appallingly extensive. How much more did he know? Please God, not enough!

'Yes.'

Her curt response didn't stop his probing as he leaned back again in his chair. 'You must be looking forward to it after such a very long engagement? And only four days to go until death do you part. No wonder you look slightly…emotionally ragged. It's going to be a big church wedding, I understand. I'm amazed you could spare the time to dash down here…or was this a welcome distraction from the bridal jitters?'

Vivian lifted her chin and gave him a look of blazing dislike. At the same time she lifted her champagne glass and took a defiant sip.

He watched her with a thin smile, and suddenly she had had enough of his subtle tormenting. Any moment now she was going to lose her temper and give the game away. Thinking, In for a penny, in for a pound, she closed her eyes and recklessly quaffed the whole lot. It really was glorious, like drinking sunshine, she decided, drenched in a fizzy warmth that seemed to invade every body-cell.

She was still feeling dazzled inside when she re-opened her eyes and found him regarding her with serious consternation.

'You shouldn't knock Dom Perignon back like water!'

Well, she had certainly succeeded in changing the subject! She gave him a smile that was almost as blinding as her hair. 'I thought that was the way you were supposed to drink champagne. It gives such a delicious rush! I think I'll have some more.' She held out her glass.

His jaw tightened. 'One glass is more than sufficient for someone who claims not to drink very much.'

'But I like it. I want another one,' she insisted imperiously. 'A few minutes ago you were trying to ply me with wine, and now you're sitting there like an outraged vicar. More champagne, *garçn*!' she carolled, waving the glass above her head, suddenly feeling marvellously irresponsible. She might as well get thoroughly drunk before she met her fate.

'Vivian, put the glass down before you break it!' he ordered sharply.

'Only if you promise to fill it,' she bargained, crinkling her eyes with delight at her own cunning.

He looked at her silently for a moment, during which her body began to take on a slow lean in the chair. 'All right.'

She chuckled at him. 'You promise?'

'I promise.'

'Cross your heart and hope to die?'

'Vivian—'

'Stick a needle in your eye—!' She broke off the childish chant, putting her free hand to her open mouth, her face blanching under the freckles. 'Oh, God, Nicholas, I'm sorry.'

'The glass, Vivian—'

She was too shocked at her thoughtlessness to register anything but her own remorse. 'Oh, Nicholas, I didn't mean it, I was just being silly. You mustn't think I meant—'

'I know what you didn't mean, Vivian,' he ground out, as she regarded him owlishly from behind her spectacles.

'I would never tease you about your eye,' she whispered wretchedly.

'I know,' he said grimly, lunging to his feet and reaching for her glass just as her limp fingers let it go. It slid past his hand and shattered on the stone-flagged floor into hundreds of glittering shards.

'And now I've smashed your lovely crystal,' she said mournfully, her eyes brimming with more tears at the knowledge of the beauty she had carelessly destroyed. 'You must let me buy you another one.'

'By all means pay for the glass. You've smashed a hell
of a lot worse in your time. Perhaps it's time you were
made to pay for that, too,' he growled, and caught her
just as she toppled off the chair, bumping her cheekbone
on the edge of the table.

'Oh!' Her back was arched across his knee, her head
drooping over his powerful arm, hands flopping uselessly
to the floor. 'You've gone all wavy and soft,' she murmured dizzily.

'Your glasses have fallen off.' His voice came from
such a long way away that she had to strain to hear it.
Her thoughts seemed to flow stickily through her head,
oozing aimlessly like melted honey and slurring off her
tongue.

'Why won't my arms move? What's happening to me?'

'Perhaps you're drunk.'

She felt a warm weight slide under her knees and then
the whole world went around and she gave a little cry as
she seemed to float up towards the heavy-beamed ceiling.

'I don't think so. I never get drunk.' The rocking feeling didn't make her feel sick, as the boat had. She was
being carried, she realised muzzily, struggling against the
dragging desire to melt into the arms that held her against
a hard chest.

'What's happening, where am I going?' she slurred
weakly.

'Wherever I care to take you,' came the terse reply.
'Don't you know what you've done, Vivian?'

She had used to know, but somehow the knowledge
was now wispily elusive. 'No, what have I done?' she
mumbled.

'You've pricked yourself on a thorn, a very dangerous
kind of thorn...'

'Poison.' The word floated up through her subconscious

without fear. 'Was it poisonous? Am I dying now...?' It was much nicer than she expected, she decided woozily, aware of a strange, shining whiteness all around.

'No, damn it, you're just going to sleep. You're only drugged, not poisoned.'

'Must've been a rose-thorn, then,' she said, having trouble getting her silly tongue around the words. There was a flat, echoing, metallic rhythm coming from somewhere close by, keeping time with the rhythmic rocking that was making her float higher and higher away from reality. Confusing images clouded in her wandering brain. 'Was a rose, wasn' it...tha' caused all th' tr'ble? In B-Beauty an' the Beast...'

'You're getting your fairytales mixed up, Sleeping Beauty.' The bitter steel of his voice cut into her fading consciousness. 'I may be a beast but my name's not Rose—it's Thorne, Nicholas Thorne.' His grip tightened and he shook her until her bewildered green eyes opened, staring fiercely down at her.

'You do remember my name, don't you, Vivian?' he burst out harshly. 'Even if you never saw my face. Nicholas Thorne. The man you almost destroyed ten years ago. The Olympic athlete whose future you smashed to bits with your car?'

She stirred weakly in his arms. 'No...!'

'The man whose wife and son died while you walked away with hardly a scratch,' he went on relentlessly. 'Do you believe in the Bible, Vivian? That justice is an eye for an eye...?'

She rejected the horror of what he was implying, the black eye-patch suddenly dominating her hazy vision. Perhaps he intended that it was the last thing she would ever see! Frantically she tried to bring her hands up to hide her face, to protect her eyes from his avowed revenge, but they, like the rest of her body, refused to respond to orders.

'*No*!' She was falling now, with nothing to save her. He had thrown her from the high place into a pit of horror. She was falling down, down, down and he was falling with her, his breath hot on her face, his unmasked hatred and the formidable weight of his hard body pressing her deep into the soft white oblivion that was waiting to receive them.

'Ssh, I've got you.'

Her body twitched feebly. '*No...*'

'Fight it all you like, Vivian, it's too late,' he murmured in her ear, with the cruel tenderness of a murderer for his victim. 'All you're doing is hastening the drug's absorption into your system.' His hand was heavy across her throat, his thumb pressing against the sluggish pulse under her jaw as his voice deepened and roughened. 'You may as well accept that for the next few hours I can do whatever the hell I like with this voluptuous young body and you won't be able to lift a finger to stop me. Would Marvel want you back, I wonder, if he knew that someone else had grazed in these lush pastures?'

Strangely, the lurid threat with its menacingly sexual undertones didn't terrify her as it should have. To be ravished by a man who could make her tingle all over with just a look didn't seem such a bad thing. She was sorry she would miss it. She might even have said as much, for as her eyelids seeped closed for the last time she heard a soft, incredulous laugh.

Her last conscious awareness was of his mouth warm on hers, his tongue sliding intimately into her moist depths, a leisured tasting of her helplessness as large hands began smoothing off her clothes.

And the sound of someone wishing her sweet dreams.

CHAPTER FOUR

WHEN Vivian opened her eyes she was still trapped in the fuzzy white wilderness.

She blinked, and discovered that she was lying in an incredibly soft, warm bed and the whiteness was the curving surface of a wall a few inches from her nose. She reached out to touch the rough plaster surface, using the contact with reality to push herself upright, meaning to peer out of the narrow window which broke the curve of the wall at the end of the bed. Instead she sank back on her heels with a smothered moan as her head swam horribly.

'Poor Vivian. Head thumping like a drum?'

She opened herself mindlessly to the warm sympathy in the sugar-coated voice. 'Umm...' she groaned in inarticulate agreement.

The sugar melted to sickly syrup. 'Hangovers are a bitch, aren't they? I had no idea you were such a reckless drinker. I told you champagne shouldn't be knocked back like water...'

Vivian swung around on her knees and froze, uttering a gasp of shock as she discovered why the bed was so blissfully warm.

'*You!*'

'Who did you expect? The faithful fiancé?'

Nicholas Thorne was sprawled beside her, his solid outline under the covers blocking the only escape-route from the narrow single bed. His tanned shoulders were dark against the stark white pillows and his chest above the folded sheet bare, apart from a thick dusting of gold-flecked body-hair that didn't soften the impact of the powerful slabs of raw muscle. Even lounging indolently in bed he managed to exude an aura of barely leashed strength. His head was propped against the stout slats of the wooden bed-head and, with his tousled blond hair and scarred beauty, and a mockingly cynical smile on his lips, he looked to Vivian like the epitome of sin—a fallen angel begging for the redemption of a good woman...

It was a shockingly seductive thought and she wrenched her eyes away from their forbidden fascination with his body, all too aware that his expression of sleepy amusement was belied by the tension in the muscles of his arms innocently resting on top of the bedclothes, ready to thwart any foolish lunge to freedom across his body. Not that she was in any condition to make one. She could hardly think, over the riot in her head. She rubbed a hand across her aching eyes and gasped, suddenly realising what was so different about him. He wasn't wearing his eye-patch.

'You have two eyes!' she blurted out.

'Most people do,' he said drily. 'But, in my case, one is strictly non-functional.' He angled his head so that she could see the immobility beneath the distorted left eyelid, the clouded iris.

'H-how did it happen?' she whispered shakily.

'You have to ask?'

She closed her own eyes briefly. 'Yes, it seems I do. They told me at the time that your injuries weren't serious—'

'I find that hard to believe.'

Her eyes flew open at his harsh scepticism. 'I was only

fifteen! Still a minor as far as the law was concerned—nobody told me very much of anything. The police dealt mostly through my parents—' She broke off, realising the dangers of her impulsive self-defence. 'But you can't blame Mum and Dad for wanting to protect me,' she protested quickly. 'They were just doing what any parents would have done in the circumstances...'

In fact, they had been so anxious that she should not be traumatised by the tragedy that they had shielded her from all publicity surrounding the accident, and most of her concrete information had come from that dreadful night at the hospital where, still in a state of shock, she had been gently questioned by a Police Youth Aid officer. She was told that the pregnant front-seat passenger of the other car, Mrs Barbara Thorne, had been thrown out and killed instantly when it rolled down a steep bank. The driver, Nicholas Thorne, had suffered concussion and leg injuries. His son, who had been belted into a back seat, had also miraculously escaped without life-threatening injury.

The car-load of boisterous teenage party-goers, including fourteen-year-old Janna, that Vivian had been driving home along the gravelled country road had suffered only shock and bruises.

To her relief he didn't pursue the point. Instead he stroked a finger across his scarred lid and said simply, 'Fragments of flying glass. This was slashed to ribbons, although fortunately my sight seemed to have suffered only temporary damage. But an infection set in a few months later. A microscopic sliver of glass had worked its way through to the back of the eye...'

And here she was moaning in self-pity over a mere headache! 'And...your leg?'

'Not as bad as the limp might suggest. I can do pretty well everything on it that I used to.'

'Except run.'

Several days after the tragedy she had overheard part of a low-voiced conversation between her parents in which her father had said it had been a twin celebration for the Thornes that night—Nicholas's twenty-fifth birthday and the announcement that his sprinting had earned him selection to the New Zealand Olympic team.

'Oh, I can still run. Just not like a world-class sprinter,' he said, in a voice as dry as dust.

'I see...' She might as well plough on and remind him of *all* the dreams that meeting her on a rainy road that night had crushed. 'And...you never married again?'

'No.'

The clipped reply said more than all the rest. 'I'm so sorry,' she said, her voice crushed with guilt and compassion.

His expression tightened dangerously, then relaxed as he studied her gravity, the sincerity of the pain-glazed green eyes and tragic freckled nose. His gaze flickered over her kneeling figure, and he smiled with sinister intent that curled her toes.

'How sorry, I wonder?'

'Wh-what do you mean?' She put a hand up to her pounding head, overwhelmed by the impossibility of dealing with his unpredictability in her debilitated state. One moment he seemed charming, almost gentle, the next he was brimming with black-hearted villainy.

Maybe she wasn't even awake yet at all. Maybe this whole ghastly week was just one, ultra-long, insanely bad dream...

'Having trouble concentrating, Vivian?'

'My head...' she muttered, hating herself for showing such weakness in front of him.

'Perhaps you'd like some hair of the dog? Champagne seems to do wonders for your mood. Makes you very...co-operative.'

Vivian stiffened. 'It wasn't the champagne, it was whatever vile stuff you put in it,' she growled raggedly.

'You mean the chloral hydrate?' He met her accusing glare without a flicker of remorse. 'I assure you, it's a very respectable sedative—the drug of choice for a whole generation of spy novels. Hackneyed, perhaps, but very effective: tasteless, odourless, highly soluble and fast-acting. You might feel a little hung-over for a while, but there won't be any lasting physical effects—at least, not from the *drug*...'

She wasn't up to interpreting any cryptic remarks. She was having enough trouble trying to establish the most obvious facts.

'Where am I, anyway?' she croaked, looking around the small, cheese-wedge-shaped room.

'The lighthouse. I'm in the process of having it converted into living-space. In fact, you might say this is the penthouse suite.'

Vivian winced as his words reverberated like a knell of doom inside her fragile skull. She lifted her other hand and massaged her painfully throbbing temples, desperately trying to remember how she had ended up in bed with her worst enemy—a man who ten years ago had accused her of murder and Janna of complicity, in words that had burned the paper on which they were written with their vitriolic spite.

Her fingers pressed harder against the distracting pain as she asked the question that should have been the first thing out of her mouth.

'What are you doing here?'

'If you mean physically, rather than existentially, at the moment I'm just enjoying the view.'

He wasn't referring to the window behind her, Vivian realised, as his gaze slid several points south of her pale face, where it settled with a sultry satisfaction that made her belatedly aware of a growing coolness around her upper body.

She looked down, and gave a mortified shriek as she saw that her chest was as bare as his—more so, since she didn't have a furry pelt to cloak her firm breasts, thrust into lavish prominence by her unconsciously provocative pose. All she had to hide behind were her freckles, which were scant protection from his mocking appraisal. In the split second before Vivian whipped her arms down, she was shamefully aware of a tightening of her pointed nipples that had nothing to do with the invisible caress of chilled air.

Flushed with humiliation, she snatched at the bedclothes, tugging the sheet up to her face as she cringed against the rough wall behind her. Outrage burned away her drug-induced lethargy as her blush mounted. All the time that they had been talking, Nicholas Thorne had *known* that Vivian was unaware of her semi-nudity. While she had been seriously struggling to communicate, he had been encouraging her to flaunt herself like a floozie, savouring the anticipation of her inevitable embarrassment!

She skimmed an exploring hand down under the covers and found to her deep dismay that all she had on were her tiny bikini panties.

'What happened to my clothes?' she demanded furiously, sweeping a blurred look around the room. The bed, a small bedside cabinet and a strange, triangular clothes-horse in the centre of the room appeared to be the only furniture. No closet or clothes, masculine or feminine, appeared in evidence.

'Don't you remember taking them off?' he asked, shifting to fold his arms casually behind his head, his leg brushing her knee under the covers and making her jump.

'No, I do not!' she gritted back fiercely. 'I remember *you* taking them off.'

Her fingers tightened their grip on the sheet, her eyes blazing green fury above the white veil of cotton as it all came rushing back in vivid detail. He had been kissing her, gloating over her helplessness, and it was only because of his insidious drug that she hadn't fought him tooth and claw!

But she wasn't helpless now, she thought grimly. He wanted a run for his money and that was what he was going to get!

After all, that was the reason that she had knowingly walked right into the jaws of his meticulously baited trap.

Her plan was beautifully simple: by presenting Nicholas Thorne with his prime target at point-blank range, she would draw his fire long enough to exhaust or at least appease the machiavellian lust for vengeance that was compelling him to treat anyone and anything that Vivian loved as a pawn to be used against her.

'Did I?' His surprise was patently mocking. 'Goodness, how shocking of me. Are you sure it wasn't just a wishful fantasy?'

'The last person I would want to fantasise about is *you*!' She whipped the sheet down to her chin, raking him with a look of furious contempt. She was prepared to take anything he dished out, as long as he left her family alone. The success of her whole mission hinged on his never finding out that she was a willing self-sacrifice.

'You lured me here under false pretences. You drugged me and took off my clothes!' she hissed at him goadingly.

'Only the ones that were superfluous to requirements,' he replied blandly.

'What in the hell do you mean by that?' She bristled like a spitting ginger kitten, all kinds of wild scenarios exploding through her scandalised imagination.

'What do you think I mean?' He stretched the arms behind his head languidly, expanding the impressive structure of his chest as he murmured tauntingly, 'Are you wondering whether those sexy emerald-green panties are a tribute to my gentlemanly honour...or to my sexual ingenuity?'

Since it happened to be exactly what she was thinking, Vivian reacted furiously. 'In the circumstances, I hardly think the question of *honour* arises,' she said scathingly.

'You may be right,' he stunned her by replying. He came up on one elbow and Vivian reflexively jerked the covers more securely around her.

Unfortunately, her hasty movement tugged the coverings away from the other side of the bed, exposing Nicholas's long, muscled left flank, lean hip and rippling abdomen. The skin was slightly darker on his half-raised leg and thick torso than on his hip, the naked swimsuit line jolting her with the knowledge that, while she might be semi-nude, he was totally naked!

Thankfully his modesty was preserved by a vital fold of sheet, for Vivian's wide-eyed attention lingered for a startled moment before being hurriedly transferred to his face.

'Some parts of me are fortunately still *extremely* functional,' he purred, his undamaged eye glinting with a predatory amusement. 'Especially in the mornings...'

'*Mornings*?' Vivian's hot face swivelled gratefully

away from him towards the soft yellow-pink glow at the window. 'But...it's sunset,' she protested in weak confusion. 'It's just getting dark...'

'Actually, it's getting light,' he corrected. 'That window faces east, not west.'

Vivian sucked in a sharp breath as the full implication of what he was saying hit her. She hadn't just lost a mere hour or two. She had already spend half a day and a whole night entirely at his mercy!

'Quite so,' he said softly. 'This is the morning after, Vivian. Which, given the fact that we're in bed together, naturally poses the deeply intriguing question: the morning after *what*?'

Vivian stared at the thin, sardonic curl of his mouth that hinted at depths of degradation she hadn't even considered.

'Oh, my God, what have you done?' she whispered fearfully, her body shivering with the disgraceful echo of a half-remembered thrill.

'More to the point, what *haven't* I done?' he murmured wickedly, pivoting on his elbow in a fluid flow of muscle to retrieve something from the bedside cabinet behind him.

He offered it to her and, when she refused to let go of her flimsy shield of bedclothes, let a cascade of coloured rectangles spill on to the rumpled fabric between them. Her back glued protectively against the wall, Vivian frowned stiffly down, afraid to move, and frustrated that the surface of the bed was just beyond the range of her near-sighted focus.

'Here, perhaps these will help.' He sat up in a flurry of bedclothes, ignoring her automatic cringe as, moments later, he pushed her spectacles on to her wrinkled nose. 'Better?'

It was a hundred times worse! Vivian stared, appalled, at the photographs scattered like indecent confetti over the bed.

'Oh, my *God*...!'

'It's a little too late for prayers, Vivian. Your sins have already found you out. Quite graphically, too, wouldn't you say?'

'How...? I... You—'

He interrupted her incoherent stammering smoothly. 'I would have thought that the *how* was self-evident. There's this clever modern invention called photography, you see...'

The sarcastic flourish of his hand made Vivian utter a soundless moan as she saw that what she had myopically mistaken for a clothes-horse was in fact a tripod, topped with a fearfully sophisticated-looking camera, its lens pointing malevolently at the bed.

'And as for the I and you, well—we appear to be pretty brazenly self-evident, too, don't we? Here, for instance...'

Vivian's hypnotised gaze followed his pointing finger. 'See the way you're arched across the bed under me, your arms thrown over your head in abandoned pleasure...'

Vivian clamped the blankets rigidly under her arms, freeing her trembling hands to try frantically to push his away as he sorted through the collection and selected another.

'But this one is my own personal favourite, I think. So artistic...so erotic...so expressive. Don't you agree that we make a sensuous contrast of textures and patterns? With your ginger-dappled skin and my deep tan, and the way our bodies seem to flow over and around each other...'

Vivian tuned out his honeyed taunts, transfixed by the searing image suspended from his fingers.

She had seen raunchy advertisements for perfume in glossy women's magazines that were more physically revealing, but it was impossible to be objective now. The couple in this photograph weren't anonymous models posing for public display. That was *her* caught in an attitude of utter abandon, that was *his* nude body aggressively crushing her to the bed. She went hot and cold at the idea that he had somehow tapped into her forbidden desires.

Even as a tiny, clinical voice of reason was pointing out that the alignment of Nicholas's fingers on her hip conveniently covered the precise area where the thin strip of her bikini panties would be, Vivian was shattered by a sickening sense of betrayal. The pictures lied; they depicted an act of violation, not of love!

She tried to grab the photographs out of his hand and, when he laughed jeeringly and held it out of her reach, she fell desperately on the others, tearing them into meticulously tiny pieces, all the while trying to protect her threadbare modesty with the slipping covers.

He laughed again, making no attempt to stop her wild orgy of destruction beyond retaining safe possession of his avowed favourite. 'There are plenty more where those came from, Vivian. It was a very long, exhausting night...'

'I was unconscious,' she panted, rejecting his sly insinuation. 'Nothing happened—' She stopped, stricken. 'My God, you were going to do this to *Janna*?'

'Actually, the original plan was for someone else to play your sister's partner in sin,' he drawled. 'And when they supposedly disappeared together, with the payment for the land, I would send you photos of the lovers and evidence that they had planned the fraud together. You were supposed to come dashing to her defence on the eve of your own wedding, sadly too late to rescue the contract that your company was depending on, but in plenty of time to negotiate the salvage of Janna's personal and professional reputation—at the price of your own, of course...

'Your arriving in Janna's place sabotaged the exquisite complexity of the plan, but I'm nothing if not flexible. As soon as I saw you, I knew I wanted the privilege of handling you to be purely mine...'

She had already guessed much of it, but the callous detachment with which he outlined the bare bones of the plot was chilling.

She gasped, as an even more horrible thought smacked her in the face. 'Who took the photos? Who else was in here, watching us—?' She broke off, shuddering with humiliation at the thought that Frank had been a flint-eyed witness to her degradation...

'I can promise you, Vivian, you weren't seen or touched by anyone but me.' He took a small black wafer of plastic from the table by the bed and pointed it towards the tripod, pressing a button so that she could hear the electronic whirr as the flash momentarily dazzled her eyes. 'Remote control. It's a state-of-the-art instant camera— the photos only take a few minutes to develop.'

He rolled off the bed and Vivian uttered a choking cry, closing her eyes a fraction of a second too late to deny herself a glimpse of taut male buttocks and hard, hair-roughened flanks.

'Prude.' His mockery singed her burning ears. 'Here.'

She peeped warily through her lashes and relaxed a trifle when she saw that he had pulled on his jeans. He was holding out the thin red sweater he had worn the previous day.

He shook it impatiently at her immobility. 'Come on.' He threw it on the bed. 'Put that on.'

'I want *my* clothes,' she said stubbornly, as she watched
him apply his eye-patch, raking his thick, blond-streaked
hair over the thin band of elastic that held it in place.

'Then want must be your master.' He put his hands on
his hips, legs aggressively astride, a bare-chested pirate.
'Or rather, *I* shall—and as your master I'm quite happy
for you to remain without clothes indefinitely. In fact, yes,
I rather like the idea of keeping you here naked...' He
invited her to consider the notion in a dark, seductive
voice, watching her defiance waver. 'Nude, you'd be so
deliciously vulnerable, so much easier for me to control...'

With a muttered curse, Vivian snatched the sweater and
hastily pulled it over her blushing head, contorting herself
to arrange it carefully over the top of the bedclothes before she let them go. Thankfully, the sweater came to mid-
thigh, although she still felt horribly exposed as she
crabbed to the edge of the bed and swung her feet tentatively to the floor.

'That colour makes you look like a fire-cracker with a
lit fuse.'

The faint suggestion of approval confused her. She was
acutely conscious of the scent of him clinging to the
sweater, mingling with her own, and of the soft brush of
the thin fabric against her bare breasts. She licked her
lower lip, and then fingered it nervously. It felt fuller than
usual.

'What are you going to do—with the photographs, I
mean?'

'Why, there's only one honourable thing *to* do with
them.'

Hope flared briefly. 'What's that?'

He plucked her hand from her mouth and mockingly
kissed the backs of her fingers.

'Have them delivered to the church on Saturday, of
course. Your poor fiancé must be given some reason for
being left stranded at the altar!'

His tongue flicked against her knuckles, stroking her
with a brief sting of moist fire that distracted her from his
bombshell. She jerked her hand away, but not before he
had caught her wrist and with a savage twist removed
Peter's ring from her finger.

'We'll send this bauble along with the pretty pictures,
just to make sure he gets the message that he can't have
you.'

He tossed it in the air and caught it, flaunting his possession before thrusting it casually into his pocket.

'You can't do that...' Vivian whispered, her first
thought of the havoc he could wreak on an already tense
situation, that was, if the wedding hadn't already been
cancelled. Had Janna and Peter taken her advice seriously
and gone ahead with the arrangements, or were they still
stubbornly wallowing in joint guilt and remorse?

'Marvel will never marry you now, Vivian. Learn to
accept it.'

'No, Peter loves me!' she declared desperately, jumping
to her feet. On one level, at least, it was still true. It was
because of his deep affection and respect for Vivian that
he and Janna had put themselves through such torture over
the past few weeks. Vivian hadn't even been able to maintain a righteous fury over the betrayal, for it was obvious
that the guilt-stricken pair had suffered agonies trying to
ignore and then deny their love, in order not to hurt sweet,
gentle, defenceless Vivian.

She had bluntly told them to stop being so nobly self-
sacrificing. The practical thing to do would be to forget
the huge hassle of calling off the elaborate wedding-
arrangements and returning all the presents, and just

switch brides. Janna and Peter had looked so appalled that Vivian had burst out laughing. It had been the laughter more than anything that made her realise that perhaps she wasn't as heartbroken as a jilted woman should be.

So, when the first opportunity had presented itself for her to prove that she wasn't the sweet, gentle, defenceless creature everyone was going to feel sorry for, she had grabbed at it defiantly with both hands.

'Marvel's going to take one look at those pictures and know it's all over between you.' Nicholas continued his ruthless attack. 'He'll never be able to forget the sight of you burning in your lover's arms—'

'We're not lovers!' Vivian shrieked. 'Those pictures—they're all fakes. You just... You posed me, like a *mannequin*—'

'Did I really, Vivian?' he taunted softly. 'You were very willing. Don't you remember telling me how I made you feel all soft and hot and buttery inside, and grumbling that it wasn't fair you had to miss out on the thrill of being ravished by a sexy villain...?'

'That was the drug talking, not me! There's a big difference between being barely conscious and being *willing*,' she pointed out with smouldering force. 'And—and, anyway—if I... If we *had* done anything...I'd *know*...'

'How?' He seemed sincerely curious.

She practically melted her spectacles with the glare she gave him. 'I just would, that's all,' she said stubbornly.

'Not if I was *very* skilful and very tender, and you were very, very receptive... Not if you were all soft and buttery inside,' he said, in a satin murmur that slithered over her skin.

'Stop it! I won't listen!' she cried childishly, covering her burning ears with her hands. His eyes dropped to the sharp rise of the hem of his sweater as it flirted against her upper thighs, and she hurriedly lowered her arms. 'No one else will listen to your lies, either. They'll believe *me...*'

'But you won't be there to tell them the truth,' he said smoothly. 'You'll be here with me. You don't think I'm going to let you go so easily, do you?'

'But you have to let me leave eventually.' She tried to sound confident.

'*Eventually*, you may find that you don't *want* to leave...'

His insinuating murmur filled her with alarm. What was he suggesting—that he intended to turn her into some kind of...*sex*-slave, addicted to the forbidden pleasure that he could provide?

'You can't keep me imprisoned here forever...' she protested faintly.

He shrugged. 'Who's keeping you prisoner? You came here of your own free will. In fact, you've already sent a fax to your office saying that everything is fine and that you'll be back with the contract the day before the wedding. So don't think anyone's going to come flying to your rescue.'

That much was true. She had been too secretive, too determined to solve the problem herself.

When she had gone to visit Nicholas Rose's lawyer, to plead that her sister's illness made it impossible for her to deliver the settlement papers personally, as arranged, Vivian had been still reeling from what she had discovered on her visit to Janna's flat.

Then she had bumped into a secretary over-loaded with files, and glimpsed among the scattered papers a letter addressed to Nowhere Island—but to Nicholas Thorne, not Nicholas Rose.

Some fast and furious digging for information had

brought answers that had shocked her out of her self-pitying depression and sent her charging off in a spirit of reckless bravado.

Only now was she realising how ill-prepared she was for her mission. Nicholas Thorne had shown no sign so far of being open either to intimidation or to reason.

Vivian swallowed. Damn it, she couldn't afford to let negative feelings undermine the determination that had brought her here!

'Look, I realise that you genuinely feel that you have some justification for hating me, but don't you see that what you're doing is *wrong*. That car crash was an *accident*. The police investigated it thoroughly at the time—'

'Your sister claimed that our car skidded as we came around the corner,' he said neutrally.

'Yes, but Janna wasn't *accusing* you of anything,' Vivian explained eagerly. 'She was just describing what she saw. The police said the skid-marks confirmed that neither of us was speeding…it was just the way the gravel had been shifted by the rain, making the road unstable—an act of God…'

Then she added gently, because she knew the tortuous ways that guilt could haunt the innocent, 'Neither of us was to blame for that night. Not me and not you. We'll never know if we could have prevented it by doing something slightly faster or reacting differently, but being human isn't a *crime*…'

She broke off because he was looking at her extremely oddly. 'You think I blame *myself*?'

She hurriedly changed her tack. 'When I wrote to you back then, I just wanted you to know that I was sorry for the accident…I didn't mean to taunt you with your grief, if that was what you thought. I—I never showed your reply to anyone else. I didn't think you meant those terrible threats. I thought it was just your grief lashing out. I can't believe you've nursed that mistaken grudge all these years. Surely, for the sake of your son, you should have put the tragedy behind you—'

'My *son*?'

The floor suddenly seemed to heave beneath her feet as Vivian realised what his arrested expression could mean. 'I—I know he was injured, and it's all a bit hazy now, but at the hospital I remember the doctor saying he was a very lucky boy to be in the back seat... H-he *is* still alive, isn't he?'

He nodded slowly. 'Very much so.'

'Oh. *Oh*! That's great!' Vivian's eyes were starry with brilliant relief. 'And...in good health?' she asked, with more restrained caution.

'Excellent.'

She beamed at him. 'I'm so glad for you!'

He cocked his head with an ironic smile. 'So am I.'

'It must have been a terrible experience for a child,' she said, her emotions swinging wildly back to deep compassion.

'At fifteen, you were little more than a child yourself.'

She drew herself up to her full height, once more unsettlingly conscious that the top of her head barely reached his unshaven chin. 'I've always been mature for my age.'

'You like children?' he asked inconsequentially.

'Of course I like children,' she said, bewildered.

'Some women don't.'

'Well, I *love* them,' she said firmly. She lifted her chin defiantly. 'Peter thinks I'll make a great mother.'

His eye narrowed. 'From what you know of me, you should be on your knees begging for mercy, not deliberately going out of your way to annoy me,' he warned with silky menace, and she gasped as his big hand suddenly curled around her throat, applying an uncomfortable pressure to draw her towards him until her breasts rested against his chest.

'Take your own advice, Vivian, and forget the past. You're not going home to marry Marvel; you're not going to have his children or share any kind of future with him...'

His hand tightened under her jaw, lifting her up on to her toes, so that she had to clutch at his thick shoulders for balance, her fingers sliding against his smooth skin.

'I'm your future now. I'm the one who controls your destiny.' She gave a little yip as his free hand slipped under the hem of his sweater to splay warmly across her quivering, tautly stretched belly. 'And I'm the one who controls your fertility. The first child you'll ever carry in your womb will be *mine*. The first baby to suckle at your breast will belong to *me*, as you will...'

Vivian trembled in shock at the starkly primitive statement of possession and her equally primitive response. Her lips parted soundlessly as his fingertips skimmed under the lacy band of her panties and pressed gently into the fringes of the downy thicket between her thighs.

'Such a fiery little nest... Is it as hot and spicy as its colour suggests? I'll bet it is...' She gave a faint whimper that was stifled by the nip of his teeth against her tender lower lip and his purred praise vibrating over her tongue. 'I bet you're hot and spicy all over when you're in sexual heat, peppered with those delicious freckles and salted with the sweat of your arousal. I look forward to dining on your splendour...' His hand moved up to brush briefly across the silky undersides of her heavy breasts, pausing to discover the betraying tightness of her nipples.

He made a deep sound of male gratification and suddenly released her, stepping back to study with ferocious pleasure her swaying body and her dazed look of sensual confusion.

His chest rose and fell rapidly, his body rippling with arrogant satisfaction as he straightened her glasses, which were fogged and slightly askew.

'You do see the exquisite justice of it, don't you, Vivian? An eye for an eye is such a paltry vengeance for a man of my sensual nature. I prefer a much more intimate, pleasurable and *fruitful* form of revenge...'

CHAPTER FIVE

'LOST something, Ginger?'

Stomping out of the dilapidated old boat-house, which it had taken her half an hour to break into, Vivian stopped dead.

Yes, my sanity, she wanted to say. She must be mad to allow him to play these games with her; crazier still to be enjoying it.

Nicholas Thorne had threatened her in the most elemental way a man could threaten a woman, and yet it wasn't fear that made her heart race and her stomach churn whenever he was near...

She looked up, squinting against the slanting rays of the setting sun.

He was leaning against the corner of the salt-encrusted wooden building, a familiar, infuriating smile of mockery twisting his narrow mouth, an oilskin jacket flapping open over his grey fisherman's sweater and the usual pair of jeans. Somehow she had difficulty picturing him in a conventional suit, yet he must wear one all the time in his role as ruthless head of a sprawling business empire.

'A boat, perhaps?'

'You have to have one somewhere,' she growled, disturbed as ever by his wicked humour. 'You can't live on an island without owning *some* kind of boat.'

'Feel free to look around,' he replied with another quirk of his lips.

'Thank you, I will,' she said cuttingly.

She was glad she was muffled up in the bulky knitted jumper and her green woollen trousers for around Nicholas she was uncomfortably aware of her body. It was the way he looked at her—complacent, possessive, *knowing*...

At least she had clothes to cloak her self-consciousness. After staking his nerve-shattering claim on her womb, Nicholas had calmly directed her to her suit, blouse and bra lying crumpled under the bed and led her, clutching them in a bundle, down the iron stairs to the room below, where she had found her empty briefcase and the small suitcase she had left back at the motel at Port Charles. It held only toiletries, her nightdress and a single change of clothes, but it was enough to give her a slight sense of false security.

The sweater she was wearing, however, was his, reluctantly accepted as a necessity if she was to tramp around the island in the blustery weather and not die of exposure. It had amused him to lend it to her, just as it amused him to follow her around so that she couldn't just sneak off and *pretend* to search for an escape, she had *actually* to do it, thoroughly exhausting herself in the process. He was always hovering, offering irritatingly helpful suggestions and teasing her with intriguing little titbits of information about himself that increased her curiosity about him to a dangerous craving.

The more that she found out about him, the more Vivian's compassionate heart whispered that Nicholas was basically a good man whose fixation with brutal revenge was a cry from the wilderness of his frozen emotional landscape. He had found the loss of his beloved wife and unborn child unacceptable, so, in the nature of a competitive man used to winning, he *hadn't* accepted it, and the long years of denial had formed a barrier against natural healing.

In order to save herself, Vivian had realised that she would first have to save him...

'Poor Vivian,' he commiserated. 'Three whole days of scouring every nook and cranny and you still haven't succeeded in finding a way off the island. When are you going to give up?'

'Never!' She pushed past him and began stalking back up the uneven path from the rocky cove.

'Stubborn wench.' He was close on her heels. 'Maybe you should try offering bigger bribes. Frank was quite offended by the low price you put on his loyalty.'

She snorted. His number-one henchman had proved to be predictably incorruptible, but Vivian had known she was expected to go through the motions. She put her nose in the air, and promptly stumbled and teetered on the edge of a sharp, jagged incline.

A powerful arm whipped round her waist, dragging her back against him. Instinctively she reached behind her to clutch at the sides of his coat, her shocked breath rasping in her throat.

'Don't worry, I won't let you go,' he said, wrapping his other arm around her. 'You're safe.'

She felt his face nuzzling into the side of her neck, the stubble of his jaw pleasurably rough against her skin, and for a moment she leaned weakly against him, tempted by his gentleness.

'Safe? That's a laugh! I won't be safe until I get home!'

'Oh, yes, I bet you feel boringly safe with Marvel,' he said mockingly. 'Two years engaged to the man and your dossier says you never stay overnight at his flat. I'd say that indicates a pretty huge lack of excitement on both sides—'

'Just because I'm not promiscuous it doesn't mean I'm sexless!' she flashed from the depths of her insecurity, deeply resenting his familiarity with the private details of her life.

'I don't think you're sexless, just surprisingly unawakened,' he told her smoothly. 'But I wake you up, don't I? You rise so beautifully to the slightest hint of bait. No wonder you're so gullible—you're tough on the outside and marshmallow within. A delicious bundle of contradictions...'

'*You* can talk,' she said, bristling at the gullible label.

'Oh, do you find me delicious, Vivian? I'm so glad it's mutual.' He smiled archly. 'Would you like another sample?'

'No, thank you!' she lied tightly. That searing, sensuous first kiss in his room had also been his last. His dark threats of sexual domination had made her lightning-swift response to his touch all the more shaming, and yet he hadn't pressed his advantage.

Braced for further brutally expert assaults on her deplorably shaky defences, Vivian had instead been left at the mercy of her own fevered imagination. This subtle form of self-inflicted torture had been refined with an added sadistic twist by Nicholas—she was still forced to share his bed every night.

The first night Vivian had searched everywhere, and been forced to accept that he was telling the truth when he said there were no extra beds. When she had tried to curl up fully-clothed on the couch in the living-room of the keeper's cottage, Nicholas had simply slung her over his shoulder and borne her off to his room in the tower, coolly telling her that she could change into her nightdress in privacy, or he would strip her himself and she could sleep with him naked. She had chosen dignity over humiliation and then lain on her side facing the wall, stiff with mingled rage and agonised apprehension as she felt him get in behind her.

Then—nothing!

He had whispered goodnight, tucked his arm comfortably around her middle, yawned and gone to sleep. She had tried to wriggle out from under his arm, but in sleep he was just as possessive, his hand sinking more securely under her waist, a thick, hair-roughened thigh pushing between her knees to drape over her leg, anchoring her firmly against the bed. Even through her blessedly modest nightgown she could feel the warm shudder of his heartbeat against her back and the firm definition of his manhood pressed against her soft bottom.

Each succeeding night it had taken her longer to fall asleep, and each morning when she woke up in a confusion of blushes it was to find that some time in the night she had turned over and mingled with him in a trusting sprawl of limbs.

To her chagrin he accepted her rejection with a careless shrug. 'I came to tell you that Frank almost has dinner ready,' he said. 'And I've already warned you it's not a good idea for you to be stumbling around out here alone when it starts to get dark. Look what nearly happened just now—'

'That was because you were distracting me. Maybe you did it on purpose,' she goaded, inexplicably angry at him for caring. 'Or maybe you'd like to see me go over a cliff, to be killed by an "accident". That would be rough justice for you, wouldn't it?'

In the waning light his features were blurred into softness, his eye deeply shadowed by his fierce brow. 'Do you really think I brought you here to kill you?'

'I... No,' she admitted truthfully. His declared intent

had been to cause her maximum mental suffering and she couldn't suffer if she was dead. 'But we both know there are worse things than dying...'

He moved closer. 'Like bearing my child, you mean? Would that really be a fate worse than death, Vivian? To make love with me and create a new life...?'

The wind snatched her breath away. 'You only said that to frighten me,' she choked. 'I know you weren't really serious— '

'Do you? Just because I haven't mentioned it again?' He captured her gaze with the bold assurance of his glittering brown eye. 'I knew I didn't have to. I knew you were thinking about it every time you looked at me— wondering what it would be like to accept me as your lover. Wondering if I would make love with the same passionate intensity with which I seem able to hate. I was giving you time to get used to the idea. After all, there's no real urgency now that you're here, living, eating, sleeping with me. I've waited this long for you...I can wait a little longer...'

A *little* longer? Heat suffused her body at his arrogant sexual confidence. She fought to cool her instinctive response. How could she feel anything but revulsion at his depraved suggestion?

She shivered. 'Surely you wouldn't use force to—to—'

'Not force—seduction,' he said smoulderingly. 'We both know that there's been some very volatile physical chemistry brewing between us since the moment we met. Why don't you just accept that we were always fated to become lovers?'

Fate again. Wasn't that the very thing she had come here to defy boldly? Vivian shivered once more.

'You're cold—why didn't you say so?' Nicholas scolded her, shrugging impatiently out of his jacket and wrapping her in the heavy oilskin, tucking her chilled hand firmly through his elbow as he escorted her back along the stony path towards the cottage. 'You should have worn the parka I offered you. No sense in cutting off your nose to spite your face. And if you're going to go storming around in a temper, watch out for the wild-life—they have first priority. Nowhere Island is a wildlife sanctuary and part of a maritime park. All these outlying islands are really the tops of drowned hills, and the eroded volcanic tubes that riddle the shore and sea-floor make very rich habitats for marine life.'

'You sound like an environmental tour-guide,' she said grumpily, trying not to respond to the enthusiasm in his voice.

'I should hope my learning is a little more useful than that,' he said drily as he opened the back door. 'As a marine biologist, I don't approve of environmental tour-ism.'

'What!'

He pushed her stunned figure over the threshold of the kitchen, where Frank was cursing over a sizzling pan.

'You're a property developer!' she accused, as he whipped his jacket from around her shoulders and hung it on the back of the door.

'I'm also a marine biologist. It *is* possible to do more than one thing with your life, Vivian. One doesn't have to limit oneself to living down to other people's expec-tations,' he said softly. Was that a dig at her?

He pressed a finger against her jaw, pushing it closed with a slight snap. 'What's the matter, Ginger? Aren't I fitting into your stereotype of a grief-crazed vengeance-seeker?' He stepped away. 'I'm going to have a quick shower before dinner.' The dark gleam of light reflecting off his eye-patch managed to give the startling impression

of a wink. 'Feel free to join me if you want to help con-
serve the tank-water.'

As soon as he was out of the room, Vivian turned to
Frank.

'Does he really have a degree in marine biology?'

'Yep. An athletic scholarship in the States.'

She waited but, as usual, further information was not
forthcoming.

'You don't talk much, do you?'

'Don't have much to say.'

She would have been offended if she hadn't discovered
that he was almost as taciturn in his communications with
Nicholas. She hadn't quite worked out Frank's job de-
scription yet; he seemed to be a combination of assistant,
valet, bodyguard, mechanic—he had already fixed the
faulty back-up generator—and chief cook and bottle-
washer.

'Where's Nicholas's son?'

He shrugged. 'Ask Nick.'

'He won't tell me. He won't talk about his son at all.
Or his wife.' She gave a little huff of frustration. 'How
long have you worked for Nicholas? Did you ever meet
his wife? Do you know what she was like?'

That brought the hawkish face around, bearing a hard
stare.

'Six years. No. Beautiful.'

It took her a moment to realise he had actually replied
to all her questions. She sighed. 'I thought she must have
been.'

Astonishingly Frank's dour expression broke up in a
grin.

'Nothing like you.'

She scowled. 'OK, OK, you don't have to rub it in. She

was so perfect he's never met another woman to match up to her.'

'Is that what he told you?' His grin widened and she studied him with suspicious green eyes.

'What's that supposed to mean?'

He shrugged. 'It's your life—you figure it out.'

And, with that irritating observation, he crouched down to open the oven and stir something inside.

Vivian was about to demand a proper answer when her eyes fell on a bulge in the front pocket of the jacket hanging against the door. She remembered the weight of something bumping against the side of her knee with a vaguely familiar chink as Nicholas had hurried her along. His keys! She had searched all over the lighthouse, but there was one place she hadn't been able to look.

She darted silently over and boldly plunged her hand into the pocket. Fisting the key-ring, she just had time to nip back to the other side of the room before Frank closed the oven and turned around.

'Uh, I think I'd better go and change for dinner,' Vivian said uncomfortably, edging out of the door.

Her heart was in her mouth as she crept down the hall. The plumbing in the lighthouse was still incomplete, so Nicholas would be showering in the cottage bathroom and probably had his fresh clothes with him, which meant he wouldn't need to go back to his room before dinner. Even if he did, the locked room was on the fourth landing, and she would have plenty of time to hear him on the stairs and whip up to the next level to fossick innocently in her suitcase.

The locked door hid exactly what she had suspected: an office. A businessman with Nicholas Thorne's autocratic reputation would never trust anyone enough to relinquish control of his business, even temporarily. She pulled the door softly to, and switched on the light.

There was a computer work-station and various unidentifiable pieces of electronic equipment, and a big desk strewn with papers.

Vivian ignored the wall of shelves lined with jars and tubes of dubious-looking specimens, her heart sinking at the sight of the heavy steel combination-safe on the floor.

She went over to the desk. Only the top drawer was locked and she rifled quickly through the others, finding mostly stationery and files of scientific papers and journals. Nothing that might tell her more about Nicholas the *man*. No stray photographs of his wife or son. No photos of any other kind either...

Adrenalin spurted through her veins and her sweaty hands shook as she unlocked the top drawer and sat down on the big swivel chair behind the desk to reach inside.

The first thing she touched was a small medicine bottle, and her fingers tightened around the amber glass as she picked it up and read the typed label: chloral hydrate. Her soft mouth tightened and she pushed the half-full bottle into her trouser pocket, intending to dump the contents at the first opportunity.

Her heart gave a nervous convulsion when she saw what the drug had been sitting on—the settlement contract, signed, witnessed, dated—intact and still viable...

She lifted it out and weighed it in her hands. But no...even if she took it, where could she hide it? The fact that Nicholas hadn't already destroyed it was surely a hopeful sign. As long as it lay here undisturbed, Marvel-Mitchell Realties still had a future.

She put the contract back, her breath fluttering as she slid it to one side and saw her forlorn dis-engagement ring crowning one very distinctive, disturbingly erotic photograph. She tried not to look at the haunting image, afraid to touch it lest she become further victim to her depraved fascination with Nicholas Thorne.

But where were the others Nicholas had taunted her with? The wedding was supposed to be the day after tomorrow. If only she could continue to stave off disaster until the ceremony was over! She didn't want her wedding-present to Peter and Janna to be a bunch of pornographic photographs and a threat of financial ruin. She could just imagine the poor vicar's face if he caught a glimpse of any of those pictures. She would never be able to hold up her head in church again!

However much she longed to believe that her brief presence here had taken the edge off Nicholas's bitterness, had softened and changed him, she didn't dare take the risk of relying on her increasingly biased judgement where he was concerned. Only when Janna and Peter were safely and securely married would Vivian let herself take the gamble of trusting Nicholas, telling him the truth and hoping that he would justify her faith in his basic humanity.

She scrabbled frantically through the drawer, reaching deep into the back where she found something firmly wedged. She pulled it out.

A cellphone. She flicked a switch. A *working* cellphone.

Civilisation was only a single telephone call away.

The alternatives bolted through her brain in the space of a split second. She didn't have to go through with it. She could call Peter—call the cops. She could cause a scandal. Make a great deal of misery for everyone concerned, but save herself.

And perhaps drive Nicholas out of her life forever...

She let the telephone clatter back into the drawer at the

same instant that she became aware of another presence in the room.

She hadn't heard him on the stairs and now she saw why. His feet were bare as he crossed the uneven wooden floor, not making a sound. He wore only a white towelling robe and his hair drifted in damp clumps across his brow.

He was breathing hard. And he was angry.

'Careless of me.' Nicholas leant over and slammed the drawer viciously shut, nearly catching her guilty fingers in the process.

'And even more careless of you to be caught.' He locked it and wrenched the keys out with a violent movement. Vivian slid out of the chair and nervously backed away.

'What were you doing, Vivian?' he demanded harshly, stalking her every move. 'Snooping? Or were you frantic to get to a phone so you could warn Lover-boy?'

The back of her thighs hit the computer table and she pulled her scrambled wits together as he halted, his whole body bunched with furious aggression.

'*No!*' His appearance had rendered her split-second decision redundant, but she wanted him to know what it would have been. 'No. I—I didn't even know there was a phone in here. I was just looking for the photos—the other ones you said you had—'

'I also said you were gullible,' he sneered. 'The only photos I had, you tore up—except for my personal favourite, of course...' He wasn't wearing his eye-patch and even his sightless eye seemed to blaze with sparks of angry golden life as he smiled savagely at her bitter chagrin.

'I was thinking of having it blown up and framed before I send it to Marvel,' he taunted. 'It'll have so much more impact that way. Perhaps I should even call him myself, give him a blow-by-blow account of how much pleasure I got from having his chaste bride-to-be *mounted*...'

She flinched at the crudely insulting *double entendre*. His volcanic rage seemed wildly out of proportion to the condescending amusement, even wry admiration, with which he had greeted her other failed attempts to thwart him.

'OK, OK, so I took the keys because I wanted to steal from you and snoop among your secrets,' she flared, fighting back with her own fortifying anger. 'I thought I might find something I could use to help persuade you to let me go. What's so terrible about that? *You* snooped through *my* life—'

He stiffened, his expression hardening to granite.

'And, tell me—if I suddenly agreed with everything you said? If I handed you your precious settlement contract and said all debts were cancelled—what then? Would you be able to walk away and forget that any of this ever happened? Would you still marry Marvel on Saturday?'

For a heartbeat Vivian ached to be selfish and trust to his sincerity. 'Why don't you let me go, and find out?' she said warily.

She knew instantly that she had made a serious mistake. His jaw tensed and colour stung his cheekbones as if she had delivered him a sharp slap across the face. Oh, God, had the offer been genuine?

'I wouldn't tell anyone, if that's what you mean,' she said quickly, hoping to repair the damage. 'Nobody back home has to know about any of this. It's still not too late—'

'The hell it isn't!' Turning away from her, he jerked his head towards the door and grated, 'Get out!'

Was he ordering her out of the room, or his life? She moved hesitantly past him. 'Nicholas, I—'

He sliced her a sideways glance of fury that stopped
the words in her mouth. 'Frank said you were changing
for dinner. Don't make a liar out of him.'

Then his voice gentled insidiously. 'And, Vivian...?'
Her fingernails bit into her palms as he continued with
dangerously caressing menace, 'If I ever catch you here
again, you won't find me so lenient. Be very careful how
much further you provoke me tonight. I'm in the mood
for violence...'

'If I ever catch you here again...' He wasn't sending
her away! Vivian was shocked by the turbulence of her
relief as she shakily made her way up to the room where
she kept her meagre selection of clothes.

Deciding it might be deemed further provocation not to
obey his thinly veiled command, she quickly put on a
fresh blouse, the cream one she had worn the day of her
arrival, and changed her sneakers for her low-heeled
shoes. The trousers, she decided with the dregs of defiance, could stay—she could do with their warmth around
her woefully trembly knees.

The kitchen had been transformed in her absence. It
was no longer a bright, practical workplace; it was a shad-
owy corner of a private universe, lit only by twin flickering candles set on a table laid for two. A casserole dish
sat in the centre, flanked by a bottle of red wine and two
glasses. Nicholas, she discovered with an upsurge of her
heartbeat, was still wearing his white robe—a spectral
white phantom floating at her out of the darkness.

'What happened to the lights?' she asked sharply.
'Where's Frank?'

There was a brief gleam of teeth from the phantom and
a movement of his head so that she could see that the
dark triangle of his eye-patch was back in place, his vulnerability well-masked. 'I'm conserving generating

power,' he said, in a tranquil tone of reason that sent a frisson down her spine. His silky calm was like the eye of a hurricane—she could feel the energy swirling around it. 'And Frank's already eaten. He's in his bedroom. Why? Did you want him for something?'

The innocent enquiry made her seethe. He knew damned well why she wanted a third person present! Frank was no use as a buffer tucked away in his little concrete bunker down the hall.

It was pure nerves that made her blurt out as she sat down, 'I'm not sleeping with you tonight!'

He sat across from her, leaning his chin on his hand so that his face moved forward into the flickering pool of light, his eye gleaming, a tiny candle-flame dancing like a devil in the hot, black centre. 'What's so different about tonight?'

She was hypnotised by the devil. 'It just is, that's all.'

'Do you mean that you're more aware of me as a man than you were last night?' he murmured.

She didn't think that was possible! 'An *angry* man,' she qualified stiffly.

'I've been angry with you before. Usually you just fling my temper back in my teeth.'

'Usually you behave with more self-control.'

His smile was darkly knowing. 'Maybe it's not *my* lack of control that you're worried about. Don't you trust yourself in bed with me any more, little fire-cracker? Afraid I might have lit your fuse?'

Her soft mouth tightened and he laughed softly, reaching across the table towards her. Vivian stiffened, but he was only removing the lid from the casserole.

'You dish up the food. I'll pour the wine.'

'Oh, but I don't know if I like red wine—'

'You'll like this one. It's a gold-medal winner from a

vineyard I part-own in Gisborne,' he said, brushing aside her diffidence as he filled her glass. He poured himself a glass, drank half and refilled it, all in the time it took her to ladle some of the steaming casserole on to their plates.

She waited until she had eaten several mouthfuls of food before she took her first sip. In spite of her determination not to react, she was unable to prevent a murmur of surprised pleasure as the full-bodied flavour exploded against her palate, drenching her senses in its heady bouquet.

'You see, you never know whether you're going to like something until you try it. You need to be more adventurous, Vivian, experiment more...'

She didn't like the strange tension in him...nor the dangerous ease with which he broached the bottle as they both pretended to eat. She noticed he had shaved since their confrontation in his office. It had been necessary for him to shave but not to *dress*? She felt a strange thrill of fear.

'Weren't you afraid?' he said disconcertingly, his deep, hushed tone seeming to weave itself into the darkness. 'The only locked room in Bluebeard's castle... Weren't you afraid of the horrors you might find in there when you stole the key?'

'This isn't a castle and you're not Bluebeard,' she said, resisting the powerful vision he was slyly conjuring out of her imagination. 'You've only ever had one wife,' she said deliberately. 'And I'm certainly in a position to know that you didn't murder her.'

He looked at her broodingly over the rim of his glass. 'Ah, yes, my beloved wife. Frank tells me you're curious about her...' Vivian was suddenly certain that Nicholas was building up towards some kind of critical release of the tension that raged in his face, seethed in his restless eye.

'I'm in the mood for violence...'

She rubbed her damp palms surreptitiously against her thighs and felt the forgotten bulge in her trouser pocket.

The idea sprang into her mind full-blown. Her fingers closed around the glass bottle warmed by her thigh.

'I wouldn't mind a drink of water, please.'

He got up, moving with his usual swiftness and precision, and Vivian knew that in spite of the wine he had consumed he was still dangerously alert. It was only his inhibitions that had been relaxed, and thus the bonds that chained his savage inner demons.

The moment he turned away to the sink, she pulled out the chloral hydrate, wrenched off the lid and tried to shake a few drops into his full wine glass, horrified when the clear liquid came out in a little gush.

She didn't have time to get the bottle capped and back into her pocket, and had to thrust it down on her lap as she accepted her glass of water, feeling the remainder of the drug soak into the fabric over her hip as her heart threshed wildly in her chest.

'You wanted to know about Barbara...'

She watched, her green eyes wide with fascinated horror, as he re-seated himself and took a long swallow of his wine before he spoke again. Oh, God, what madness had possessed her? What if she had given him too much and he died?

'The biggest mistake of my arrogant young life...'

Mistake? Vivian was jolted out of her frantic abstraction.

His mouth twisted at her expression. 'You thought it was the love-match of the century? Mis-match, more like. It was my father's idea. He's an extremely dominating man and I'm his only son, his greatest pride—and his greatest disappointment. We clashed on just about everything. When I came back from university overseas, he was very ill and used some very clever emotional blackmail to pressure me into marriage with his god-daughter. Needless to say, he then miraculously recovered.'

'Then…you fell in love with each other after the marriage?' Vivian said, her thoughts falling into chaos.

'Love was never part of the equation. Like my father, Barbara saw our marriage in terms of status and control. We lived separate lives from the start. She politely endured me in her bed because it was necessary in order to secure her permanent place in the Thorne dynasty—part of her bargain with my father, I gather—and I politely endured for reasons just as selfish, because I wanted nothing to disturb my build-up for the Olympic trials…'

He paused and Vivian held her breath, hoping the fascinating revelations were going to continue.

'Then Barbara told me she was pregnant and I realised just how permanent was the trap my father had planned for me. Except it wasn't—the next day she and the baby were killed…'

He reached for his wine-glass again and Vivian couldn't stop a darting gesture of involuntary protest.

'Oh, no, please don't drink that!' She clumsily tried to knock it out of his hand.

'Why not? Are you afraid I'll pass out on you before I finish baring my soul?' He stopped, his face sharpening as he looked from her stark expression of appalled guilt to his glass, his shrewd brain making the impossible leap in perception.

'My God, is there something wrong with this? *What have you put in my wine?*'

He lunged across the table with a roar, scattering the

burning candles, and Vivian's chair crashed over as she jumped to her feet, sending the empty bottle in her lap spinning to the floor.

She didn't wait to see him recognise it. She fled.

She flew down the hall and crashed through the door into the lighthouse in a blind panic, triggering the sensor lights in the stairwell. She was thundering up the stairs before she remembered there were no locks on the doors, nowhere to hide. It was too late now; she could feel the pounding vibration of his mysteriously delayed pursuit through the steel under her flying feet.

He caught her just below the fourth level, not even attempting to stop her but merely gathering her up in his furious momentum, driving her onwards and upwards with the bulldozing threat of his body. Only when they reached the landing of his room did he actually lay a hand on her, catching her right wrist and using their combined speed to swing her away from the stairs and through the doorway, shoving her back against the wall, anchoring her there with the full thrust of his body, slamming his other hand on to the light-switch so that she was exposed to the full glare of his rage.

'How much did you give me?' he snarled, his breath fogging up her glasses, his lips brushing hers in an angry parody of a kiss. 'The whole damn bottle? How *much*, damn you?' He rattled her against the wall.

'I don't know—a little, a teaspoonful, I don't *know*!' she panted desperately. 'I spilled the rest of it, that's why the bottle was empty. I'm sorry, Nicholas, I panicked, you were frightening me...' She was begging now, but she was beyond caring. 'Please, I'm sorry—'

'*Sorry!*' he ground out. He shook his head violently, as if the drug was already beginning to affect him.

'Maybe you should sit down before you fall down,' she said, feeling wretchedly weak herself.

'Maybe I should,' he said thickly. He pulled her away from the wall and dragged her over to the bed, pulling her between his spread legs as he sat down, fumbling in his bath-robe pocket. She felt a cold metallic clasp replace the heat of his hand on her wrist, and looked down just in time to see him snapping the other handcuff around his own wrist.

'My God, what are you doing?' she asked numbly, staring at their shackled limbs. So this was why she had got such a head start on his superior strength and speed. He had gone to get *chains*!

'Making sure you'll be here when I wake up,' he said grimly. '*If* I wake up.'

She shuddered. 'Don't say that! Please, Nicholas, where's the key? You don't need to do this. I promise I'll stay…'

For an answer he fell diagonally back on the bed, throwing his shackled right wrist forcefully out to his side so that she was brought tumbling down on top of him with a soft scream of terror. He pulled off her glasses and tossed them on the floor in a careless gesture that she found paradoxically even more threatening than his violence.

'Nicholas, no…' She struggled to find purchase with her knees against the mattress, conscious that she was straddling him, and the towelling robe was parting over his powerful thighs.

'Nicholas, *yes*!' He pulled her head down, crushing her mouth against his, wrapping his right arm across her back so that her captive arm was forced behind her. He kissed her until she tried to bite him, and then he nudged her face aside with his jaw and sank his teeth into her vulnerable throat. She cried out, struggling weakly as he began to suckle at the bite, murmuring words against her skin that sapped her will and created tiny shocks of pleasure deep in her feminine core. He began to kiss her again, and this time she didn't fight him and the forceful thrust of his tongue gentled to a slow, seductive glide that made her tremble with yearning.

'I may pass out, but not before I've had a taste of you...not before you've given me everything I want...' His mouth moved to the other side of her throat, nibbling and sucking with tender savagery as his hips and thighs began to undulate beneath her. 'I'm going to devour every lovely inch of you...use my lips and teeth and tongue on you in ways that you've never even imagined...brand you all over with my mark so that anyone who looks at you will know you've come from my bed...'

Vivian knew he was talking about Peter. Briefly surfacing from her passion-drugged state, she tried to arch away, but Nicholas shifted his hand from the back of her neck to the front of her silk blouse, slipping his fingers into the prim neckline and ripping it open with a single downward stroke that scattered the pearl buttons like lustrous tears across his chest.

'Nicholas!'

Her gasp was lost in a spasm of violent sensation as he flicked open the tiny plastic catch between her breasts and allowed them to tumble free of the confining lace. The ginger freckles were stretched over their swollen fullness, the soft pink tips swaying against the hard contours of his chest, contracting instantly into tight points that scraped and caught on his own peaked masculine nipples.

His chest heaved and he uttered a harsh sound, violently tilting his hips to roll her on to her side and then her back, hefting her up against the pillows, rising up and over her on his braced hands. In almost the same motion he loosened the belt of his robe so that it fell open around her, baring the full length of his body to her restless gaze. He was hugely aroused and shuddering with a fierce tension, for all the world as if she had given him an aphrodisiac instead of a sedative.

He looked triumphantly down at the lavish bounty he had exposed, his nostrils flaring as he caught the enticing scent of her body, and recognised the subtle signals of her arousal.

'Yes—*Nicholas*,' he ground out. 'Not Peter, *Nicholas*. Admit it. You couldn't give a damn about him when you're with me!'

He cupped her breast with a possessive movement of his manacled hand, the narrow chain connecting their wrists dragging in a cold caress against the skin of her ribs as he moved deliberately, his fingers contracting and relaxing, his thumb rubbing against the rigid nipple.

He bent his head and his tongue darted out to curl around the tip he was cherishing, dragging it up into his mouth, moistening it with tender care then releasing it to the cool night air.

'You don't love him; you don't want to marry him.' The words were muffled by her flesh. 'You don't want to cling to your safe, unadventurous past...you want the fierce excitement only I can give you...you want this... and this...' He held her pleasure-drenched gaze as his mouth closed over her, slanted softly, sucked lightly, twisted, lifted and lowered again...

'I'm...not...the one who won't let...the past go,' she panted, biting her lip as he repeated the voluptuously unsatisfying action over and over, clenching her chained hand helplessly against her side, groaning with sweet agony as he finally used his teeth and suckled her with the rough urgency that she needed, marking her as he had promised with his erotic brand of possession. Her extravagant response made him explode into action, pushing heavily between her thighs, moving jerkily on her as if the fabric between them didn't exist, as if he was already buried deep inside her, pleasuring them both beyond imagining...

'Say it, Vivian...stop holding yourself back...stop pushing me away.' She was suddenly aware of a settling heaviness in his body as his head sank down on her shoulder. 'Don't let me go down into this damned darkness without a prayer...'

'Stop talking about dying!' she cried frantically, tugging at his hair to try and keep him awake.

'I'm not talking about dying, I'm talking about living. I can't let him get you... Gotta keep you with me,' he said with a blurred illogicality that Vivian knew from experience was the drug tightening its grip on his mind, but she sought to drag him back to her with desperate words of truth.

'Peter won't ever get me because he doesn't *want* me, damn you. Do you hear me, Nicholas Thorne? You were right. I don't love Peter and Peter doesn't love me. He loves my *sister*. It's *Janna* he's going to marry on Saturday, you big, gullible oaf, not me!'

For a moment he remained still, a dead weight, and she thought he had lapsed into unconsciousness, but then he suddenly rolled off her in a tangle of white towelling.

'What did you say?'

The face beside hers on the pillow suddenly looked completely wide awake. But no, his pupil was almost a pinpoint. He was conscious through sheer force of will.

She moistened her lips and nervously tucked her blouse across her breasts one-handed as she said in a husky little voice, 'I cancelled our engagement last week. But not the wedding. You see, I found out Peter and Janna had fallen in love, and, well—they were sort of mired in the inertia of their guilt. They didn't deliberately set out to hurt me, and I realised I hadn't ever really been in love with Peter, not the way that Janna is. So I told her to go ahead and get married in my place and I'd dance at their wedding.'

She smiled to show how bravely she had accepted the crushing blow to her feminine pride, but the smile began to waver under his sombre stare and, to her horror, her eyes began to fill.

'I suppose now you're going to tell me I got what I deserved,' she whispered, and burst into a flood of tears.

But instead of gloating, as she had always dreaded that he would, Nicholas quietly gathered her shuddering body against his warm length and stroked her wild ginger mane, uttering soothing murmurs while she sobbed out all the wretched details against his chest.

It took a long time to expend her storm of stored-up tears, and repeated assurances from Nicholas that he had no interest in wreaking his savage revenge on her damned sister's damned wedding, before Vivian finally hiccupped herself into exhausted sleep. Only then did the man holding her allow his mind and body to go equally lax, finally relinquishing his formidable will to the powerful seduction of the drug in his veins.

CHAPTER SIX

VIVIAN took another frigid slap in the mouth and felt her throat burn with the salty abrasion as she coughed the seawater out of her lungs.

She sluggishly instructed her head to turn and her arms to rise and fall, rise and fall, in the rhythmic stroke that had won several long-distance ocean swims at the surfclub she had belonged to in her late teens.

The wet-suit that she had taken from among the diving-gear in the lighthouse storeroom was providing her with extra buoyancy and some protection against the cold, but she knew that mental stamina would be her greatest asset in the gruelling swim.

She turned on her side, checking that she was still moving in the right direction, heading towards the uneven lurch against the horizon that Frank had let slip one day was the nearest inhabited island. Thank God the weather was good and the sea not too choppy, but even if there had been a cyclone Vivian wouldn't have cared.

She had woken just before dawn and looked at the man lying next to her in a deep, drugged sleep and acknowledged with a thrill of despair that she was in love with her capricious captor.

In the space of a few days the morals of a lifetime had been swept away. Instead of drawing Nicholas into the sunlight of reason, she had been drawn into the shadows. Something dark in herself was called forth by the darkness

in him. She could protest all she liked, but all Nicholas
had to do was touch her and she melted. And he knew it.

Last night he had admitted that he had never loved his
wife. That called into question everything she had come
to believe she knew about him. It made his motive for
revenge not one of honest emotional torment, which could
be appeased, but of cold-blooded, implacable malice.

The realisation that Nicholas must have uncuffed her
before he fell asleep was merely confirmation of her bleak
theory that he believed he had won their battle of wills.
The empty steel bracelet dangling from his own still-
manacled wrist was a mute testament to his confidence in
her sexual subjugation.

Protest had exploded in her brain. *No*! She wouldn't let
him distort her love into something that she was ashamed
of. She had to be out of his reach before he woke up.
Before he could touch her again…

Fool, fool, fool, Vivian chanted inside her head, in
rhythm to her stroking through the water. To believe that
you could play with fire and not be burnt. Fool, fool…

'Little fool! What in the hell do you think you're doing?
Of all the ridiculous, theatrical stunts!'

She suddenly realised that the new voice was much
deeper than the one in her head and far more insulting,
and the loud slapping sound wasn't the rising waves hitting her face; it was the sound of oars striking the water.

Water sheeted down her face from her sopping hair,
sticking her eyelashes together and getting in her swollen
eyes as she stopped to tread water and was nearly run
down by a small aluminium dinghy rowing furiously
towards her.

Nicholas was shipping the oars, leaning over the side,
yelling, cursing, trying to grab her slippery wet-
suited arm.

Vivian swam away, coughing and spluttering as she briefly sank. When she struggled to the surface again, Nicholas was standing silhouetted against the crisp morning sky, the boat rocking dangerously. 'For God's sake, Vivian,' he cried bleakly. 'Where in the hell do you think you're going?'

Still choking on salt-water and shock, Vivian didn't bother to answer; she just pointed in the direction of the distant island.

Nicholas exploded in another series of explicit curses. 'Do you *want* to bloody drown? You can't swim that far! Get in this damned boat *now*!'

For an answer Vivian rolled over and began swimming with renewed energy. Each time she turned her head to breathe, she saw Nicholas pulling on the oars, keeping on a parallel course, his grim mouth opening and shutting on words she couldn't hear through her water-clogged ears.

Gradually Vivian's false burst of strength drained away and the next time that Nicholas veered close she didn't have the energy to pull away.

He leaned over and caught her by the zip-cord trailing from the back of her neck, forcing her to tread water as she clung to the side of the boat, gasping air into her burning lungs. 'That's enough! You've made your point, Vivian,' he said roughly. 'You want me to beg? I will: *please* get into the bloody boat. We'll talk, and then I'll take you anywhere you want me to...'

Her green eyes were enormous in her exhausted face. 'I'm not that gullible any more,' she choked, fighting her pathetic desire to trust him, even now. '*You're* the gullible one. You never fooled me at all. I knew even before I came here who you were!'

He looked thunderstruck. 'You *knew*?'

'That Nicholas Rose was Nicholas Thorne,' she threw

into his haggard face. Her frigid lips and tongue shaped the words with increasing difficulty. 'But I came anyway, because I knew that if this was some kind of vicious v-vendetta, then the only way to stop you was to confront you face to face...so I let you d-drug me...I only *pretended* to w-want to escape... Everything you did to me you were only able to d-do because I *chose* to *let* you... Because I wanted t-time to b-be with you and c-convince you that r-revenge is n-not the way for y-you t-to find p-peace...'

Her teeth were chattering so much that she could hardly get the last defiant words out, and Nicholas made an abrupt growl and rammed his hands under her arms, hauling her over the gunwale and dumping her into the bottom of the boat.

'Thank you for *letting* me rescue you!' he said sardonically. 'I take it you weren't simply *pretending* this time.'

Vivian suddenly felt blessedly numb all over. Even her bleeding heart was cauterised by the cold. 'Why?' she whispered. 'Why did you b-bother to come and get me?'

'Why in the hell do you think? Because I love you, damn it!' he snarled savagely, not even bothering to look at her as he swivelled his torso to signal with his upraised arm. Automatically following his gaze, a stupefied Vivian saw the blurry image of a white launch that looked as big as an ocean liner foaming down on them.

'Coastguard?' Her mouth seemed to have split from her mind.

'No. Mine. The *Hero*. It's been out doing a marine survey for the last few days. As soon as I found your clothes on the beach, I called her up and used her radar to track you. Ahoy! Derek! Send down that sling, will you?'

She screwed her eyes shut as she was strapped and

hauled and bundled, and passed from hand to hand like
an unwanted package until she felt the familiar arms taking possession of her again.

Nicholas carried her down a brightly lit companionway
and into a spacious white cabin, kicking the door shut
before rapidly stripping the over-large wet-suit from her
numb body.

His mouth quirked when he saw the emerald-green bra
and panties she wore underneath. His smile thawed a tiny
slice of heart. Maybe she wasn't hallucinating, after all.
Maybe he really had said it.

'My favourites,' he murmured, fingering the saturated
lace. 'Underwear that matches your eyes.' And then he
peeled them off too, smothering her protests at his rough
handling with a thick, blue towel, rubbing her vigorously
until she cried out at the pain of the blood returning to
the surface of her icy skin.

'Don't be such a baby!' he said, planting a kiss on her
blue lips as he finished a strenuous scouring of her hair,
which had turned the dripping tails to dark red frizz. 'We
have to get you properly thawed out.'

He stripped off his own clothes and walked naked with
her to the wide berth, lying down on it and mounding the
patterned continental quilt over them both as the boat's
powerful engines throttled to full power and the sky began
to whip past the brass port-hole above their heads.

'Stop cringing, this is all very scientific. I'm a scientist—I know what I'm talking about,' he said, cuddling
her close, warming her with the sensual heat of his body,
breast to breast, belly to belly, thigh to thigh. He shuddered and buried his face in her neck. 'Oh, *God*, that feels
good.'

Vivian knew what he meant. Tears of exhaustion and
confusion trembled on her still-damp lashes.

He lifted his head and kissed them away. 'I'm sorry, Ginger—first things first. If you had bothered to wait for me to wake up this morning, you would have known this already...in fact, you would have known last night if you hadn't sabotaged my good intentions. My name is Nicholas James Thorne...the Second.'

'The Second?' she whispered, bewildered. Was he suggesting they start all over again? A second chance?

'To distinguish me from my father—Nicholas James Thorne the *First*,' he said deliberately.

Her brow wrinkled soggily. 'Your father has the same name as you?'

'No, *I* have the same name as *him*,' he corrected urgently, as if the fine distinction was important. 'Just before I was born he had an illness that rendered him sterile, which was why he was so obsessive about me marrying and perpetuating the name. There are two Nicholas Thornes, Vivian, but only one was driving the car that night—my father.'

Vivian's bleached face stormed with vivid emotion as she realised what he was telling her. 'But, your son—'

His fingers across her mouth hushed her confused protest, and the riot of blood in her veins became a visible tumult that bloomed across her skin. 'I have no son. Your "boy" in the back seat was me. To the doctor who patched me up, a twenty-five-year-old probably *did* seem like a boy—he certainly seemed old to me, although he was probably only in his late fifties.

'After Barbara was killed, my father said it didn't matter that I was crippled, as long as my genes were healthy. We had endless rows about my refusal to marry again. In the end I turned my back on it all—my father, his money, the business I was supposed to take over, the whole concept of Being A Thorne. I didn't realise that after the accident his dream had become a ruthless obsession, and the obsession had developed into a dangerous fixation with you...'

Vivian struggled to sit up, but Nicholas held her down with implacable gentleness. 'Are you saying this was all *his* idea?' she asked hoarsely through her salt-scored throat.

'I had no idea what he was planning,' he said emphatically. 'Not until I paid a long-overdue duty visit last week. As usual, our discussion turned into a furious row. He suddenly started shouting the most ridiculous things...about how it was all your fault his son had turned against him and how he was finally going to make you and Janna pay for murdering his grandson. How he had waited years for just the right moment to get you where he wanted you... He was boasting about how he was going to do it when he had a massive stroke—'

'Oh, God...' Vivian's fist came up to her mouth and Nicholas eased it away, unsurprised by her horrified compassion for the man who had tried to hurt her.

'No, he's not dead, but he's in an extremely bad way,' he said sombrely, wrapping her fist reassuringly in his. His body shifted against hers, enveloping her in a fresh wave of blissful warmth.

'As soon as he was taken to hospital, I scoured his desk and files in case his incredible ravings were true. I found his dossier on you and a load of legal transactions with Marvel-Mitchell, and I got a shock to find it was actually on the verge of happening—and on Nowhere of all places—while I was scheduled to be away in Florida. Here!' His voice hardened and she felt the muscles of his chest tense as if against a blow to the heart. 'On *my* island...the place I used to come to get away from his insidious interference in my life. That was part of his sick delusion, you see,' he added tiredly. 'That he was doing this for *my* sake. So I fired the sleazy hireling who was supposed to do all the dirty work, and flew down here myself to...' He hesitated uneasily.

'To take his place?' she challenged painfully.

He leaned up on one elbow and said ruefully, 'Actually, I came hot-foot to rescue you. To apologise and try to smooth things over and explain about my father's condition—'

'Rescue me? *Apologise*? By *drugging* me and photographing me naked in bed with you and threatening to make me have your *baby*?' Vivian squawked at him incredulously. 'You expect me to believe that was your idea of *smoothing things over*?'

To her fascination he flushed, adjusting his eye-patch in the first unconsciously nervous gesture she had ever seen him make. 'Yes, well, you weren't quite naked. And, anyway, that was partly your fault.'

'*My* fault?'

'I was expecting your sister. I had intended to be very civilised and restrained and then use my power of attorney to sign the settlement contract and wave Janna a grateful goodbye, but I took one look at you and went off like a rocket.' His voice roughened as he began to play with her damp ginger curls. 'I wanted you more than any woman I've wanted in my life. I can't explain it. I just saw you, touched you, and *knew* that we were made for each other, that you felt the same, powerful attraction that I did...

'But I knew from my father's file that you were due to get married in a week, so I didn't have much time. I decided to take some drastic short cuts, use every despicable tool conveniently placed at my disposal, to keep you here and break down your resistance to the notion of breaking up with Marvel. I thought that my pretending to be my father would buy me the time I needed to build on the potent physical chemistry between us. Of course, I didn't realise that you were also doing some bidding for the same reason...' he added slyly.

She placed her hands flat against his bare chest. 'Not quite the same reason,' she teased.

To her surprise he didn't smile. 'Are you trying to let me down lightly?' he asked quietly.

She suddenly realised that she hadn't told him. She traced his tight mouth with her forefinger. 'I woke up this morning horrified to admit I'd fallen in love with you,' she said softly. 'My heart skewered on the sword of an emotional pirate. You can't blame me for choosing the deep blue sea over the devil. You should have been more honest with me from the start...'

'Like you were, you mean,' he said drily, smiling at her rueful acknowledgement. 'It may not seem like it, but I do have *some* sense of honour, you know. I wasn't going to make love to you until you asked, and I wasn't going to ask you to marry me until you'd given Marvel his marching orders.'

'Marry!' He looked amused by her shock, and she recovered quickly. 'I thought you wanted me to be your sex-slave,' she pouted huskily.

'That, too, of course,' he said, lambent flecks of gold sparkling wickedly in his eye at her sensual boldness.

He rolled over on top of her. 'And speaking of slavery...I had to be rescued from a very embarrassing state of captivity myself this morning. Handcuffed to my own bed! I had to drag it over to the door and spend fifteen minutes yelling down the stairwell before Frank heard and came up and jemmied the cuffs open for me. He'll never let me hear the end of it!'

'You should be more careful who you go to bed with,' said Vivian demurely.

His head lowered as his knee brushed between her legs. 'I will be. *Very* careful,' he murmured against her mouth. 'In future I'll only be going to bed with my fire-cracker wife.'

As she slid her arms around his satiny-hard waist and blossomed eagerly for his love, Vivian thought it sounded like a just fate for a retired pirate...

Let's Celebrate!

LOVE & LAUGHTER™

invites you to
the party of the season!

Grab your popcorn and be prepared to laugh as we celebrate with **LOVE & LAUGHTER**.

Harlequin's newest series is going Hollywood!

Let us make you laugh with three months of terrific books, authors and romance, plus a chance to win a FREE 15-copy video collection of the best romantic comedies ever made.

For more details look in the back pages of any Love & Laughter title, from July to September, at your favorite retail outlet.

Don't forget the popcorn!

Available wherever
Harlequin books are sold..

 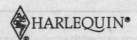

HARLEQUIN®

Look us up on-line at: http://www.romance.net

LLCELEB

Take 4 bestselling love stories FREE

Plus get a FREE surprise gift!

Special Limited-time Offer

Mail to Harlequin Reader Service®

3010 Walden Avenue
P.O. Box 1867
Buffalo, N.Y. 14240-1867

YES! Please send me 4 free Harlequin Presents® novels and my free surprise gift. Then send me 6 brand-new novels every month, which I will receive months before they appear in bookstores. Bill me at the low price of $2.90 each plus 25¢ delivery and applicable sales tax, if any*. That's the complete price and a savings of over 10% off the cover prices—quite a bargain! I understand that accepting the books and gift places me under no obligation ever to buy any books. I can always return a shipment and cancel at any time. Even if I never buy another book from Harlequin, the 4 free books and the surprise gift are mine to keep forever.

106 BPA A3UL

Name	(PLEASE PRINT)	
Address	Apt. No.	
City	State	Zip

This offer is limited to one order per household and not valid to present Harlequin Presents® subscribers. *Terms and prices are subject to change without notice. Sales tax applicable in N.Y.

Don't miss these Harlequin favorites by some of our most popular authors! And now you can receive a discount by ordering two or more titles!

HT#25700	HOLDING OUT FOR A HERO	
	by Vicki Lewis Thompson	$3.50 U.S. ☐/$3.99 CAN.☐
HT#25699	WICKED WAYS	
	by Kate Hoffmann	$3.50 U.S. ☐/$3.99 CAN.☐
HP#11845	RELATIVE SINS	
	by Anne Mather	$3.50 U.S. ☐/$3.99 CAN.☐
HP#11849	A KISS TO REMEMBER	
	by Miranda Lee	$3.50 U.S. ☐/$3.99 CAN.☐
HR#03359	FAITH, HOPE AND MARRIAGE	
	by Emma Goldrick	$2.99 U.S. ☐/$3.50 CAN.☐
HR#03433	TEMPORARY HUSBAND	
	by Day Leclaire	$3.25 U.S. ☐/$3.75 CAN.☐
HS#70679	QUEEN OF THE DIXIE DRIVE-IN	
	by Peg Sutherland	$3.99 U.S. ☐/$4.50 CAN.☐
HS#70712	SUGAR BABY	
	by Karen Young	$3.99 U.S. ☐/$4.50 CAN.☐
HI#22319	BREATHLESS	
	by Carly Bishop	$3.50 U.S. ☐/$3.99 CAN.☐
HI#22335	BEAUTY VS. THE BEAST	
	by M.J. Rodgers	$3.50 U.S. ☐/$3.99 CAN.☐
AR#16577	BRIDE OF THE BADLANDS	
	by Jule McBride	$3.50 U.S. ☐/$3.99 CAN.☐
AR#16656	RED-HOT RANCHMAN	
	by Victoria Pade	$3.75 U.S. ☐/$4.25 CAN.☐
HH#28868	THE SAXON	
	by Margaret Moore	$4.50 U.S. ☐/$4.99 CAN.☐
HH#28893	UNICORN VENGEANCE	
	by Claire Delacroix	$4.50 U.S. ☐/$4.99 CAN.☐

(limited quantities available on certain titles)

	TOTAL AMOUNT	$ _____
DEDUCT:	**10% DISCOUNT FOR 2+ BOOKS**	$ _____
	POSTAGE & HANDLING	$ _____
	($1.00 for one book, 50¢ for each additional)	
	APPLICABLE TAXES*	$ _____
	TOTAL PAYABLE	$ _____
	(check or money order—please do not send cash)	

To order, complete this form, along with a check or money order for the total above, payable to Harlequin Books, to: **In the U.S.:** 3010 Walden Avenue, P.O. Box 9047, Buffalo, NY 14269-9047; **In Canada:** P.O. Box 613, Fort Erie, Ontario, L2A 5X3.

Name: _____

Address: _____ City: _____

State/Prov.: _____ Zip/Postal Code: _____

*New York residents remit applicable sales taxes.
Canadian residents remit applicable GST and provincial taxes.

Look us up on-line at: http://www.romance.net

HBKJS97

Free Gift Offer

With a Free Gift proof-of-purchase
from any Harlequin® book, you can receive
a beautiful cubic zirconia pendant.

This stunning marquise-shaped stone is a genuine cubic
zirconia—accented by an 18" gold tone necklace.
(Approximate retail value $19.95)

Send for yours today...
compliments of ◆HARLEQUIN®

To receive your free gift, a cubic zirconia pendant, send us one original proof-of-purchase, photocopies not accepted, from the back of any Harlequin Romance®, Harlequin Presents®, Harlequin Temptation®, Harlequin Superromance®, Harlequin Intrigue®, Harlequin American Romance®, or Harlequin Historicals® title available at your favorite retail outlet, together with the Free Gift Certificate, plus a check or money order for $1.65 U.S./$2.15 CAN. (do not send cash) to cover postage and handling, payable to Harlequin Free Gift Offer. We will send you the specified gift. Allow 6 to 8 weeks for delivery. Offer good until December 31, 1997, or while quantities last. Offer valid in the U.S. and Canada only.

Free Gift Certificate

Name: _____

Address: _____

City: _____ State/Province: _____ Zip/Postal Code: _____

Mail this certificate, one proof-of-purchase and a check or money order for postage and handling to: HARLEQUIN FREE GIFT OFFER 1997. In the U.S.: 3010 Walden Avenue, P.O. Box 9071, Buffalo NY 14269-9057. In Canada: P.O. Box 604, Fort Erie, Ontario L2Z 5X3.

FREE GIFT OFFER
084-KEZ

ONE PROOF-OF-PURCHASE

To collect your fabulous FREE GIFT, a cubic zirconia pendant, you must include this original proof-of-purchase for each gift with the properly completed Free Gift Certificate.

084-KEZR

HARLEQUIN AND SILHOUETTE
ARE PLEASED TO PRESENT

Love, marriage—and the pursuit of family!

Check your retail shelves for these upcoming titles:

July 1997
Last Chance Cafe by Curtiss Ann Matlock
The most determined bachelor in Oklahoma is in trouble! A
lovely widow with three daughters has moved next door—and
the girls want a dad! But he wants to know if their mom needs
a husband....

August 1997
Thorne's Wife by Joan Hohl
Pennsylvania. It was only to be a marriage of convenience—
until they fell in love! Now, three years later, tragedy
threatens to separate them forever and Valerie wants only to
be in the strength of her husband's arms. For she has some
very special news for the expectant father...

September 1997
Desperate Measures by Paula Detmer Riggs
New Mexico judge Amanda Wainwright's daughter has been
kidnapped, and the price of her freedom is a verdict in
favor of a notorious crime boss. So enters ex-FBI agent
Devlin Buchanan—ruthless, unstoppable—and soon there is
no risk he will not take for her.

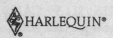 

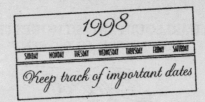

1998

SUNDAY MONDAY TUESDAY WEDNESDAY THURSDAY FRIDAY SATURDAY

Keep track of important dates

Three beautiful and colorful calendars that celebrate some of the most popular trends in America today.

Look for:

Just Babies—a 16 month calendar that features a full year of absolutely adorable babies!

1998 CALENDAR
Just Babies
16 months of adorable bundles of joy!

Hometown Quilts
1998 Calendar
A 16 month quilting extravaganza!

Hometown Quilts—a 16 month calendar featuring quilted art squares, plus a short history on twelve different quilt patterns.

Inspirations—a 16 month calendar with inspiring pictures and quotations.

Inspirations

A 16 month calendar that will lift your spirits and gladden your heart

Steeple Hill™

HARLEQUIN®

Value priced at $9.99 U.S./$11.99 CAN., these calendars make a perfect gift!

Available in retail outlets in August 1997.

CAL98